FRC

"Eloquence with an edge. In a single chapter, John Herrick can break your heart, rouse your soul, and hold you in suspense. Be prepared to stay up late."
— Doug Wead, *New York Times bestselling author and advisor to two presidents*

"A solid debut novel."
— *Akron Beacon Journal*

"Evocative ... I felt breathless ... You'll want to get this book."
— Michelle Sutton, *author of Danger at the Door*

"An inspiring story about second chances, faith and the power of family."
— Luxury Reading

"A solid read with a powerful spiritual message."
— *The Midwest Book Review*

"Herrick went where most authors fear to tread and he did [so] with a lot of grit and a lot of heart. ... He pushed the envelope and made me like it!"
— Debbie's Book Bag

"Herrick ... knows how to draw a reader in, hold your attention, and keep you guessing to the very last word."
— Examiner.com

"A well written and engaging story. It moves, and moves quickly. … I don't think I've read anything in popular novel form as good as this in describing a journey of faith."
— Faith, Fiction, Friends

"A surprising and thought-provoking read."
— A Few More Pages

"Simply bad-ass … With this book, [Herrick] breaks the mold."
— The Elliott Review

"Jesse is an amazing character, one that you can't help but love. … Once in a while a book grabs you and will not let you go; for me it is *From the Dead*. This is a literary treasure."
— Book Noise

"*From the Dead* is a stunning work. From the darkest depths of the human spirit to the light and love that surround us, John Herrick has penned an emotional, inspirational, and heart-wrenching novel."
— Minding Spot

"The issues of betrayal and redemption, selfishness and sacrifice come alive in John Herrick's *From the Dead*. … From the Dead is a realistic, dramatic, contemporary novel."
— Christian Book Previews

"Character-driven, taking the reader on a poignant and well-written journey."
— Fiction Addict

THE LANDING

A NOVEL

JOHN HERRICK

PUBLISHED BY SEGUE BLUE

Copyright © 2012 by John Herrick

Published in the United States by Segue Blue, St. Louis, MO.

Book design and layout by Jonathan Gullery
Author photograph by Pam Rempe

Library of Congress Control Number: 2008938179
ISBN-13: 978-0-9821470-0-9
ISBN-10: 0-9821470-0-7

Publisher's Cataloging-in-Publication
Herrick, John, 1975-
The landing / John Herrick.
p. cm.
LCCN 2008938179
ISBN-13: 978-0-9821470-0-9
ISBN-10: 0-9821470-0-7

1. Musicians--Fiction. 2. Man-woman relationships--
Fiction. 3. South Carolina--Fiction. 4. Love stories,
American. I. Title.

PS3608.E774L36 2008 813'.6
QBI08-600266

From the Dead excerpt copyright ©2010 by John Herrick.
All rights reserved.

PRINTED IN THE UNITED STATES OF AMERICA

To Bela,
my brand-new baby niece.

May God put dreams in your heart
and bring them to fruition.
Welcome to the family, sweet girl.

Love,
Uncle John

ACKNOWLEDGMENTS

The culmination of a twenty-year dream, *The Landing* would not have been possible without the continual source of love, encouragement, and support I've found in my family— Dad and Mom; Mike, Ritu and Bela; Tom and Sara.

Specifically, Mom read through two drafts of the manuscript. This novel stems from the advice she hammered into my brain as a child: "Do now what you'll be happy with later." Several years ago, I needed to make a change in my life, and this book marked the first step in that direction. Mom's advice helped me get there.

My brother Mike, through a genuine concern for others, makes it his habit to cheer for their success. A rare breed in this respect, I believe he seals his own success with this quality.

I am indebted to Aisha Ford, Adrian Morales and Jane Wilke for their vital input, which I've applied to all of my projects since.

Heather Manning provided pre-natal insight and served as a reader. Heather accurately describes herself as the greatest fan of my life, in an Edwin McCain sort of way.

Pam Rempe, Elizabeth Behling and Kathy Wakeman read drafts of the manuscript. Sarah Guldalian provided moral support.

Craig Perino came through at a critical time and provided marketing research to prepare this book for its launch. One friend sharpens another—Proverbs 27:17. Craig's integrity and kind heart are an inspiration. In his own words: "God has a plan."

I need to recognize Phil Lewis, who gave me my first opportunity to write for radio many years ago. I'll never forget that privilege.

All of you mentioned above, your investments in me were priceless. Thank you.

My gratitude also goes out to those I've no doubt forgotten. My apologies. You know who you are.

The process of completing a novel requires stamina and discipline. God harnessed my creative impulses through eight years in the information-technology arena, where I had the privilege of gleaning project-management skills from Rollin Pochop. To this day, I use those skills to structure my book projects and see them through to completion. Thank you.

Thanks to all the reviewers and bloggers who helped increase awareness of my work, starting with the publication of *From The Dead*.

We touch other people's lives more often than we realize. I believe in letting people know when they have touched mine. With that in mind, I would not be the writer I am today without the musical influences of Diane Warren, Bernie Taupin and Elton John. By studying their songs as a teenager, I learned the power of wrapping words around emotion and speaking to people's hearts. I have never met these writers, but one day, perhaps they will see this note of gratitude.

Thus far, 2012 has involved a lot of soul searching, reevaluation of priorities, and new consideration of what's important. I've watched prayers get answered and miracle after miracle unfold, and God has renewed the fire in my heart. In retrospect, my life contains many joys and regrets, much alone time, a lot of comfort through a lot of tears. Knowing the love of God covers me in my dark corners brings me indescribable light and warmth. In my darkest hours, Jesus was there. At night, when tears poured out as I lied in bed, Jesus was there. When I made mistakes of which I'd be too ashamed and humiliated to admit, Jesus sat beside me. He puts His arm around my shoulders, He leans His head against mine, He tells me it's all going to work out fine. When I was unwanted, I was wanted by Him. When I called myself fucked up, He called me forgiven. When God has faith in you, it changes your whole ballgame. I've never known such acceptance and unconditional love as when I soak in His presence. His love story has become mine. And for that, He has my heart forever. Because this is a mainstream novel, I was going to leave Him out of the acknowledgments, but in the end, I just couldn't do it. I'm nothing without Him; but if I have Him, I have everything. So I thank Him most of all.

Finally, thank you, readers. Of all the ways you could spend your time right now, you chose to invest a chunk of your life in this book. It's not taken for granted … I promise.

THE LANDING

PROLOGUE
CHRISTMAS EVE 1979

The star nearly toppled from its treetop perch as it rattled from the surrounding commotion.

Like a multicolored weed infestation, wads of crumpled wrapping paper lay strewn across brown carpet while kids darted across the room to show Mom and Dad their latest discoveries. As each gift received a patronizing nod of approval, the human elves raced back to conquer the next object, regaining their balance as they tripped over each other in haphazard excitement. Unwrinkled and inconspicuous, a solitary piece of paper sat toward the side of the room. Set in strategic position by a clever preschooler, it covered an eggnog stain still moist from a recent spill.

Beth Harting and Lori Bale's friendship had begun during their childhood in Colorado. And although they lived five apart nowadays, they still made frequent long-weekend visits a priority. Early on, whenever their wives had insisted on a visit, Travis Harting and Rick Bale had participated by obligation. After a while, however, the men had grown to appreciate each other's company. They had done it for their wives. They had done it for their kids. But now, they did it for themselves as well.

In addition to their three-day reunions, Christmas played host to tradition for the two families. Neither clan had relatives who lived nearby, so the Bales and Hartings had become each other's family in kind, which provided a viable excuse for a special Christmas gathering every year. Travis's employment as an assistant professor at Miami University afforded his family the opportunity to drive north for a week between semesters. And with each repetition, nothing changed except the kids, whose energy levels, like their heights, continued to inch larger.

The Bales lived in Solon, Ohio, a Cleveland suburb situated in Lake Erie's snow belts. Tonight, a steady flow of flakes fell like a blanket from the icy gray sky. The families received a serenade from Andy Williams, who, according to family legend, hid within the crevices of the stereo and crooned his seamless rendition of "Little Drummer Boy" each year.

Parked on a loveseat, Lori threw her head back in laughter as Rick explained the latest attack an anonymous prankster had concocted against his department. The epitome of a white-collar corporate lawyer, Rick had grown comfortable in his position and had managed to stay put six years and counting.

As soon as the laughter ended, Beth changed the subject.

"By the way, Lori, I still have a bone to pick with you," she said with a wink.

Rick rolled his eyes. "Ladies, this is pathetic. Give it a rest already! You do this every year."

"Beth, I didn't feed your Patty doll to the neighbor's dog," Lori said. "It didn't eat the ugly ones."

Eyes of suspicion.

"How would you know that unless you had tried to feed it to him?"

"You two are almost as bad about that incident as you are

about that football player with the zits!" Travis said.

Rick shook his head. "Travis, I'm gonna slug you for bringing that up."

"He was the cutest guy in school," Lori added. She pointed at Beth, who had sealed her mouth shut. "And she stole him from me. *Stole* him!"

"Hey, I was just trying to lure him into our little world where he would run into you more often," Beth said. "All I tried to do was add some momentum to fate, and—"

"Oh, how awful! I can't believe you stick with that alibi. Rick, would that hold up in court?"

"I hear they have clauses for it these days."

With the newest infant, Jake, in her arms, Lori turned halfway on the loveseat and peeked with curiosity at the group of rambunctious children, all less than five years old. She gestured with her head toward two of them, then elbowed her longtime friend. "Beth, look at that."

With the clumsiness of a fourteen-month-old, Danny Bale had plopped down on the floor, cozy in a blue pajama outfit with white, plastic footies. He scrutinized a sponge block, awestruck at its array of primary and secondary colors. Beside him, three-year-old Meghan Harting, enthralled with the now-walking toddler, had wandered over and taken a seat. With one arm around the boy, she guided him through the toy's facets and explained the colors like an elementary school teacher who had taken a student beneath her wing.

As he removed a tiny, salivated finger from his mouth, Danny pointed at one of the edges, squeaked a word of gibberish, then looked up for Meghan's affirmation.

"That's right, Danny!" With childlike innocence and her curly pigtails in a bounce, she squeezed a hug and pressed her head against his. As Danny continued to concoct various noises and pound the sponge block against the floor, Meghan noticed an unwrapped gift still tucked beneath the Christmas tree.

Drawn to whatever mystery might hide inside the slender box, its lure proved irresistible to her. Leaving Danny behind, Meghan wandered over to the tree and picked up the gift. She kept her eyes glued to the attraction as she held it in her hands.

CHAPTER 1
MAY 2007

Danny Bale leaned against the restroom wall, ran his finger along his wrist.

Running his fingers through his beach-blond hair, he exhaled with a heavy grunt and tilted his head toward the ceiling, the details of which he had surveyed many times before. The circles of water damage. The hole at the edge of a beige panel. An aging light bulb that had developed a mysterious, maize-colored tint. Since his arrival at Sunset Beach, this room had grown familiar. He had branded it into his memory and could re-create it with his eyes closed.

His skin was tanned, a shade between local-light and tourist-brown. Bleached by the penetrating sun, his dark blond hair had developed a bright sheen and shouted his status as a permanent beach dweller. Leaning toward the mirror, he examined the creases that had begun to form along the corners of his eyes. It seemed premature for signs of aging to begin.

Danny felt tired. He blamed it on sleep deprivation, to late nights spent writing after Sunset Beach calmed. But the root of his fatigue didn't result from poor habit or a need for a twenty-seven-hour day. Rather, a pattern of bland constancy had

emerged, leaving Danny drained at heart from years of plugging away at his craft and seeing no manifestation of success.

Not that Danny could pinpoint a definition for success.

At first, he had defined it as freedom—one he could obtain
by spending his late twenties seaside and inspired. In truth,
Danny's heart had departed for the beach long before he did.
Prior to his arrival, Danny had invested four years in the college
scene, where he had conformed to an uninspired status quo
disguised as a ladder to breakthrough. It seemed a lifetime ago.

And now, by age twenty-eight, he'd grown exhausted.

An elusive notion, success.

As he eyed his beaded necklace and linen shirt, Danny wondered how he'd managed to spend another four years of his life
at McGrady's. On weekdays and weeknights, he engaged in the
mundane work of a cook. But on weekends, McGrady's slated
him as its featured entertainment. Danny would strum his
acoustic guitar and sing the songs of Bob Dylan, James Taylor,
and some original pieces of his own. It provided Danny with a
performance outlet. And by the time McGrady's closed for the
night, Danny figured, half of the drinkers wouldn't know the
difference between songwriters anyway.

Danny jumped at the sudden burst of the restroom door.

"Danny Boy! How's it going, chief?"

Even when he dabbled with subtlety, you couldn't help but
notice Jay McGrady's presence. Forgoing college and opting
instead for a family business that would one day become his
own, Jay earned his living as the McGrady's manager and oddity
specialist. On any given day, you could spot him fixing a water
pipe or grilling a burger, taking out the trash or chewing out a
waitress. But Jay approached it all in good fun.

Danny rubbed his eyes. "Never better. I mean, you've got

the water, the ladies. This is paradise, right?"

Jay made his way to the sink and started to wash his hands. As luck would have it this evening, he would assume the role of senior chef, a title he'd created on the fly.

"Man, you should see the woman out there at table eleven," Jay said with a knowing chuckle. "Mmm, she's hot. I'll betcha she's about fifty years old, too." Flipping water from his hands, he wiped them with a paper towel until they were damp at best, then shook his head. "But that guy she's with—I don't understand it, man. What a slob! I mean, his knockers are bigger than hers, my hands were probably cleaner before I started washing 'em—and some dudes are just not meant for biker shorts, you know what I mean?"

"Geez, Jay!" Danny snickered, gritting his teeth. "I hate when you do that. I have to look at these people when I'm out there singing, you know."

"I'm serious, man! How could a woman like that be so hard up?" Jay stretched his arms toward the dingy walls surrounding him. "A prince like me and an inheritance like this place. What more could a woman want!"

"That slob probably owns a hotel down here, Jay!"

A quick chuckle and the fortunate son headed toward the door. "You coming?"

Danny nodded. "Yeah, I'm on my way."

Jay and his mouth departed as swiftly as they had burst in, and a few seconds later, Danny could hear him joking with customers in the hall. An amiable guy, you could always count on Jay for a stupid laugh. Not the intention Jay had in mind, per se, but his speech tended to accelerate faster than his tact. To his credit, the benevolent Jay was also responsible for complimentary rounds of beers among the staff, McGrady's profit-sharing program in its most primitive form. Danny, unlike the other staff members, had developed a solid friendship with Jay over time.

Pounding his fist into his other hand with determination, Danny shook the heaviness from his eyes and walked out the restroom door.

Danny didn't get far. Jay caught him by the sleeve of his shirt and tugged him toward a pair of patrons. "Guys, this is Danny Bale. He's our entertainment for the weekend," Jay said. "Danny, this is Chris Clark and Kyle Clark, two brothers I met on my way to the dining area."

Danny exchanged handshakes with Chris, the older brother, who had blue eyes, brown hair, and an athletic build. "Nice to meet you, Chris. What do you do for a living?"

"I sell document management software," Chris said. "Sales are great, but I was ready for a vacation and convinced my brother to hang out for a week at the beach."

At that, Jay gestured to Kyle with his thumb. "Kyle and I discovered we share some common ground. Tell him, Kyle."

Kyle, who had brown eyes and light red hair, chuckled. "I'm a chef in New York."

"I told him not to be intimidated by the ol' five-star establishment he set foot into here," Jay joshed.

Despite numerous attempts by competitors to challenge its dominance throughout the years, McGrady's remained the most visited restaurant at Destiny Landing, a tourist dive in the heart of Sunset Beach, South Carolina, referred to as "The Landing" by local residents. One of the first businesses to set up shop at the development, McGrady's remained the standard bearer for out-of-towner attraction, though no one could ascertain its appeal—other than the fact that it didn't *have* a niche appeal.

A catch-all establishment, management identified its clientele as casual dates and families, who would arrive sunburned in flip-flops and printed T-shirts purchased at hole-in-the-wall souvenir shops. McGrady's made no effort to impress, and its patrons sunk to meet the challenge.

With a final handshake, Danny wished them well and headed out to the dining area.

With the convergence of the dinner crowd, Danny figured the number of voices had doubled. In the narrow hallway, he nodded to a man and woman engaged in a conversation. A pair of human lobsters, their skin had burned to a wow-that-must-hurt degree. When he entered the dining area and surveyed the range of people in the audience, tiredness dissipated from his body. He sensed a rush of energy, an aggressive rise in the rate at which his blood coursed through his veins.

Danny was home.

He hummed to Dave Matthews Band's "The Best of What's Around," which blared through speakers hung years ago by two teenagers with a roll of twine and a questionable sense of safety. Perched upon metal rafters, the speakers loomed like crows over the talking customers, who ignored them. From a distance, Danny waved at a group of waitresses, tanned beauties who came to Sunset Beach during Spring Break but never bothered to return to the world of academia.

Toward the kitchen, Danny counted a handful of patrons sitting at the bar, but the majority of his audience partook of faux-rustic cuisine at the hut-shaped restaurant. Along the perimeter and throughout the midsection, he watched them eat at tables of various sizes and matching brown tint. Ashen fumes dimmed the room as they crept in a hypnotic blur beneath the overhead lights. In a front corner sat a small platform, occupied

by an empty stool and an acoustic guitar, which sat behind a
microphone. Two large speakers sat on the stage floor. Tonight
it would be Danny's stage.

As Danny walked up the steps and onto the platform, the
heat from a single row of tracking lights invigorated his skin like
a candle flame. Danny nodded at Jay, who meandered to the side
of the room and faded the music to silence. With a thumbs-up
signal, Jay departed for the kitchen, leaving Danny alone with
the crowd. Danny couldn't help but grin. Grabbing the guitar
and tossing the strap over his shoulder, he plugged the instrument into an amplifier and turned toward the microphone.

"Hey everybody, I'm Danny Bale. Welcome to McGrady's!"
When he spoke into a microphone, mysterious warmth ensued
within him. He couldn't explain its rationale, but something
about it always felt right. Unable to determine if he was bathing
the air with his voice or vice versa, he perceived a connection
with the audience and possessed a keen awareness of when it
was mutual.

The audience applauded.

"How you all doing tonight?" Glancing around and catching eyes with a few regulars, his pulse now raced. This was his
drug. "Either it's dinner time, or you all heard that Jay McGrady
wasn't your entertainment for the night."

As the audience snickered at the lackluster pun, Danny shot
a mischievous glare over at Jay, who bowed from behind the
kitchen window.

"All right," Danny said. "Let's get cooking."

With delicate care, he began caressing the guitar strings in
the key of G. On most occasions, he would launch the evening
with a classic rock song—something buzzing with adrenaline, a
personification befitting beer and hot wings. Tonight, however,

he felt inspired to start slow with a song of his own. And after a few introductory measures, he slid his hot-buttered vocals into the microphone and bore his heart. Danny inhaled the smoke-saturated air and ignited it with the sweet aroma of words on fire.

> There's something about her eyes
> I can't put my fingers on
> It's in the way she looks at me
> That keeps me oh so strong
> There's something about her eyes
> That takes the best of me
> It reaches down inside my heart
> And conquers me easily

Whenever he gazed at a crowd, he observed the reactions of those who listened. The romantic songs never ceased to amaze him, because with them he witnessed how a casual crowd could morph into a captivated audience. In reality, most customers allowed the music to sweep over their heads and into the hazy milieu. But as he studied through discerning eyes, Danny could spot his music's effect on a handful of people, who would become his core fans for the minutes that followed. He searched for subtle gestures that suggested mood alterations: a tilted head, an arm sliding around a girlfriend's waist, two eyes glimpsing past his guitar and into the depths of his soul. Perhaps his greatest compliment was the woman who failed to notice the delivery of a meal because of an undivided focus on the musical message that emanated. One by one, audience members found themselves distracted from their Friday night conversations and swept into Danny's personal world. Their attention spurred him on. Danny could see his future when he received such feedback—silent, yet undeniable.

Climaxing with a high note and free-falling to a final chord, Danny blushed as the song ended and the muted applause arose.

"Thank you," he said.

As much as he hated to do it, it was inevitable. The mood needed to be broken and an emotional balance maintained—a reminder of why McGrady's drew capacity crowds on Friday nights. After all, this was Sunset Beach, and its visitors had flocked here for two reasons: to get their senses teased and their skin fried.

Danny picked up the tempo and continued his song set as the blend of conversational tones resumed at full volume.

CHAPTER 2
MAY 2007

Her office was located on the far edge of Oxford, Ohio. Today, Meghan Harting would take her time getting there.

A quiet town about a half-hour from Cincinnati, Oxford was home to thousands of Miami University students, as well as a smattering of local residents who observed the migration of young adults to their hometown every autumn. As the community's largest source of revenue and employment, Miami had positioned itself as a force to be reckoned with. Plus, with a greater concentration on academics than a splashy athletic program, the university's football games provided an avenue for family entertainment that remained affordable.

A visitor to the town might imagine the significant slowdown the town must have experienced during the summer months. But Meghan had seen it firsthand. An Oxford native, Meghan had spent her entire life walking around campus with her dad. But these days, she found herself on site as a non-traditional, part-time student: part-time hours, part-time academic years, part-time class attendance. Since childhood, her casual attitude had surfaced much to her father's dismay, but he had grown to accept it as a distinct feature of her personality. Besides, with

Travis Harting a professor at the institution, Meghan's tuition carried a hefty discount. And perhaps she would even locate a career path in the process.

Career direction was the least of Meghan's concerns at the moment, however. Today she wanted to stroll down the campus streets and fill her lungs with a dose of medicinal life. In the last few minutes, she had overcome a minor case of nausea stimulated by the strange odor that filled some of the aging buildings. She couldn't put her finger on the cause—ointment and cotton balls or something. She shivered at the thought of it. As the sun's cozy rays lathered her hair, Meghan watched green leaves rustle from the tickle of a warm breeze. Who could rush to work on such a May afternoon?

As Meghan wandered down a side street and past a series of classroom buildings, red brick and Ivy Leaguish, she noticed the roads had become less cluttered as students returned to their hometowns after final exams. An occasional car broke the calm as it weaved and honked its way off of university grounds, announcing its arrival to the outside world.

Homes fated to decades of student leasing lined Oxford's streets. Meghan rolled her eyes at a group of howling fraternity guys who sat on their porch steps with nothing better to do than to flash "8.5" signs in her direction to rate her appearance. Meghan figured they had probably just finished drinks and pizza from the night before. She supposed they had chosen to savor their final days of boyhood jests before a white-collar world forced them to swap pizza-stained T-shirts for coffee-stained neckties. Amused at the thought, she wondered how many years these cocky guys would remain juveniles.

She shot them a look of disdain and kept walking, eventually catching a university shuttle bus bound for the opposite side of town.

· · ·

Meghan walked through the glass doors as if nothing was wrong. While her late arrival at the building wouldn't go unnoticed, she wouldn't sweat it. The Oxford Meadows apartment complex was her paycheck, not her lifestyle.

She almost collided with Bob, the office manager, who rounded a corner and rushed for the front door. A stack of paperwork beneath his arm, he glared at his watch from the corner of his eye.

"I was wondering when you'd get here," Bob sneered between pants of breath.

"My exam ran late."

"Oh, okay. I'll be back in a couple hours. Got a meeting offsite." And off ran Bob, a man on a mission and without a clue.

This job is a joke, mused Meghan.

With a glance to the corner of the office, she found the waterless fish bowl empty, which meant no one had deposited a late rent payment. No mundane data entry today.

Despite keeping watch for residents approaching the room, Taryn, the staff member on duty, had failed to notice Meghan's entrance. Engrossed in her task at hand, Taryn scissored her way through a stack of *Summer is here!* decorations that would soon don the office walls. Never a dull moment.

"Hey there," Meghan said. She tossed her book bag beneath her desk and transposed into the role of a leasing associate.

Taryn looked up, as if to downplay the fact that she had

missed an office walk-in. "How'd the test go?"

"I think it went okay. Post-Civil War American history."

"Was the class any good?"

Meghan shrugged. "The instructor was pretty cool. An old hippie, so it was a blast hearing him talk about the sixties, especially since he lived it—well, 'smoked it' is probably more like it." She sat down and reached for a file folder from her inbox. "Only one more exam to go."

Taryn offered a half-interested nod and examined the pile of construction paper through her wire-rimmed glasses. Deciding on orange this time, she began another artistic assault. According to Bob, the decorations would foster a sense of homecoming when one arrives at Oxford Meadows. But Meghan knew half of the single-parent and college-aged residents would flip the bird to sentimental fuzziness as they parted with their monthly rent checks.

Opening the folder and flipping through its contents, Meghan grimaced. "I just processed this paperwork. What was Bob thinking when he gave this back to me?"

"He said there was supposed to be an extra charge for the damage to the door post."

"Why doesn't he put a note on this stuff? I can't read his frickin' mind."

Taryn laughed. "Are you in a bad mood or just being yourself? It gets hard to tell."

"I don't have patience with stupid people."

Meghan thumbed her way through a few opened envelopes that also sat in her inbox, then carried them to the computer, a shared resource among the staff. Shared because, after all, they needed to reserve funds for construction paper and such.

"Did you end up going out last night?" Meghan asked.

"Yeah, Chad and I caught a movie," Taryn replied. "We hadn't seen each other for a few days. Two paramedics are on vacation, so he and some others have taken turns covering those shifts."

Meghan started typing. She gave Taryn a half-glance over her shoulder and asked, "Did you notice a change after you got married? Did the romance come or go?"

"I don't know, it doesn't seem like much changed. I guess I'll know better in six years rather than six months. He's a sweetie, though." Suddenly interested, Taryn leaned forward. "Why? Are you and Brian thinking about taking the big step?"

Meghan typed faster. "Oh, we've talked about it in passing," she replied. "But nothing serious. He seems content with the way things are, so I don't push it."

"How long have you been together?"

"Eight years." The words sent a shock through Meghan. How had it been that long? She recalculated the years in her head but arrived at the same figure. By the time Taryn's next question arrived, Meghan had started counting Valentine's Days.

"What do you love best about him?" Taryn asked.

Meghan couldn't recall when she'd last considered it. The answer should have been simple, but with her guard down, she was left searching for an answer. She shuffled a few papers, searching for a nonexistent lease agreement to buy some time.

But in the end, Meghan could think of just one response.

"He's never cheated on me," she said.

"With all the college girls around here, that's a big accomplishment."

While relieved she'd concocted an answer, Meghan considered the answer deficient. Taryn's question continued to linger in her mind like a rash, a relentless nag, refusing to be ignored.

Interrupting her silent struggle, a pair of high school kids walked past the office, armed with beach towels and aiming for the back door. Although close in age, one of the teens towered almost a foot above the other.

"Pool's not open, guys," Meghan shouted across the room, hoping to catch them before they wasted extra steps.

Turning on their heels, the teenagers roamed into the office, the taller one scrunching his nose as he morphed from navigator to mouthpiece. "When does it open?" he asked, his face overlaid with an expression of perpetual boredom.

"Memorial Day weekend," Meghan answered. They couldn't be older than fifteen. And there was no way they were old enough to drive.

"Can we just go out there anyway?"

"It's dry concrete."

"I know." Definitely not older than fifteen.

"Well, what do you think you're gonna do with a concrete hole and no water?" Halting, Meghan leaned back in her chair. She inspected the shorter boy's avoidance of eye contact, then added, "Do you kids even live here?"

"My friend lives in number twenty-five," the taller teenager said.

Without breaking her gaze, Meghan pointed her red fingernail at the shorter kid, who drew on the carpet with his bare foot. "Is this your friend?"

The shorter kid looked up. Wide-eyed, he all but admitted his status as a trespasser, which appeared to add more guilt to his conscience.

"No," the taller one replied, adjusting his shell necklace. "My friend's at school."

Without a hint of hesitation, Meghan shot her finger in the direction of the front door. "This isn't a park. Get out."

The shorter boy, already out the office door, appeared relieved. The taller one scratched his cropped, red hair, then turned and followed, grumbling a muffled expletive on his way out. When a slamming of the front door sent echoes down the hall, Taryn stared at Meghan.

"What?" Meghan asked, not about to justify her firmness. "They weren't supposed to be here." Case closed.

Taryn crossed her legs and cocked her head, then grabbed a permanent marker and threatened the construction paper with a black decorative flair. Restoring their conversation, she asked, "What did you and Brian do last night?"

"We had dinner. He loves a Mexican restaurant around the corner, so I agree to go once a month." Meghan examined a freckle on her arm. While she felt like an amoeba under the microscope of Taryn's third degree, Meghan didn't mind. In fact, Taryn's questions had begun to pique her curiosity. Years had cycled and recycled, and she sensed a hollowness buried within. Suddenly the once-a-month Mexican dinner seemed to personify her relationship: going through the motions, then coming back for another round, where the only thing that changed was the color of her margarita. And lately those margaritas were frozen.

While Meghan had always considered herself fearless, she now found herself in a safe zone and wondered where the comfort had crept in.

"It ended up in a fight," Meghan muttered at last.

"About what?"

"It was a stupid little thing. His cell phone rang the whole time, and he refused to shut it off one hour for dinner.

Apparently another department had worked into the evening on a project, and they needed his input on every detail. So he picked up the phone each time it rang. He does that all the time, and it drives me nuts because it's plain rude. Anyway, I got aggravated and told him to turn it off."

"He freaked out about that?"

"Well, it grew from there. We started getting into the whole career issue. He said he intends to become the top advertising executive in the industry, so it requires a lot of his time. Then he reminded me that, hey, we're not married, so it shouldn't be a big deal. I said something back, and the whole thing snowballed." Meghan squinted as her frustration resurfaced. Although she had put the scene to rest when she'd fallen asleep last night, now she found herself indulging its resurrection. Because Meghan's trust toward people had grown thin long ago, verbalizing her difficulties had become rare and overdue. Maybe Taryn could offer insight from a wife's perspective.

"Suffice to say," Meghan continued, "he wanted me to mind my own business, and that hurts after being involved for such a long time. Makes me feel like a hood ornament on his car."

Meghan and Taryn had only worked together for a few months, but conversations were frequent when a room was shared four days a week between the same two individuals. Meghan had revealed little about Brian, save a few details of a special event here and there. Taryn chewed a fingernail as if to decide whether to press forward. "Where did you two meet, anyway?" she asked.

"In Cincinnati, at this old Italian restaurant," Meghan replied. "A girl I worked with had gotten engaged, so a few of us went out to celebrate. Brian was sitting a few tables over at a dinner meeting." Meghan furled her eyebrows. "I remember thinking he didn't fit in with his group. He was dressed just like them, suit and tie, and had the same professional demeanor, but it didn't matter. Here were four guys old enough to be his father, and then there was *Brian*. He seemed to keep the conversation rolling, though.

"Anyway, his chair faced mine, and when I looked up at one point, we caught each other's eyes. Then he went back to his business conversation. A while later, I looked up again, and the same thing happened. He was cute, but I figured it was a chance encounter, nothing more.

"Eventually I stepped out into the lobby to make a phone call. Not even a minute passed before he walked through the door and said, 'Excuse me, but I couldn't help but meet you. I'm Brian Garrett.' Very polished, like he forgot to step out of executive mode. In fact, I had to giggle because he even shook my hand! Then he said he had to get back to his meeting and asked if he could take me to dinner sometime."

"Did you say yes?"

"Yeah, I decided it wouldn't hurt. What took me by surprise, though, was that he ended our conversation. He was confident—to the extreme, almost as if he had the whole thing planned and knew my answer ahead of time."

"And you said he's in advertising?"

"Yes."

"So basically, he closed the deal?"

"Kind of seems that way, huh!"

"And you kept seeing each other after that?"

"Just one date, then it went platonic. I didn't think we were compatible at all. He was wrapped up in a material world, and that never impressed me. But we got along well, and he was a good listener back then, so we became friends and talked almost every day. From time to time, he would bring up the idea of dating, but I always turned him down. That didn't deter him, because the way he sees it, 'no' is always negotiable. Finally, after five months as friends, I gave in and agreed to a second date." Meghan paused. "The truth is, before he came around, I hadn't been on a date in a long time."

Taking a seat near the computer, where Meghan had started to update invoice records, Taryn had lost interest in her construction paper. "So you stayed attached?"

Meghan shrugged. "Yeah, but it was tough. He's an overachiever. Work beckoned him constantly, so he would make dates with me, then postpone them, and I wasn't used to that." A hollow feeling settled into Meghan's gut. Or maybe it was flatness. Whatever it was, it felt eerie to her. It possessed a hint of familiarity, a long-present taunt, which she had never paused long enough to notice.

"So what kept you holding on to Brian?" Taryn asked.

Meghan thought for a moment. "I felt alone. He stood by me."

At the word *alone*, Taryn stopped asking questions. And Meghan didn't want to elaborate. For that matter, Meghan didn't know why she had chosen that particular word, but it had seemed suitable in an odd way.

Now in a daze, Meghan tried to refocus on her work. But reality had become cold pewter to her, hard and factual, like the account numbers in front of her eyes.

CHAPTER 3
AUGUST 1994

The black convertible pealed from the drive-through window, past a stop sign at 30 miles an hour, and onto the suburban street. Summer breeze sent a rush through the teenagers' lungs.

This weekend, Meghan and her brother, Greg, had driven to northern Ohio in Meghan's car, separate from their parents, as the Hartings visited the Bales in Solon. And though a year older than his sister, Greg was content to let her drive so he could keep his freshly waxed vehicle at home, safe in the confines of the garage.

For all his research and study with the university, Meghan's father could not seem to understand the logic behind the separate vehicles. To Meghan, however, her car represented more than a mere ride; with her license in hand for a year, driving had emerged as her means of escape from the plastic world of high school. Plus, she had shaved an hour from her drive to Solon, courtesy of her lead foot.

When spending the weekend together, the Bale and Harting kids had formed a tradition of leaving the house after dinner and pushing curfew as close to the limit as possible. On occasions where they crossed the line, Greg, the legal adult in the group at eighteen years old, acted as first line of defense and peacemaker between generations.

Danny, fifteen years old and without a license, welcomed the idea of freedom by association. His older brother, Reece, also relished the idea of liberty, but for a different reason. With plans to join the military after his high-school graduation, he intended to make the most of the next nine months before penning himself up in boot camp. Jake, the youngest Bale, rounded out the back seat, self-invited and self-convinced otherwise.

"Don't get trash all over my car," Meghan directed toward no one in particular as she tried to catch a glimpse of Jake's lap in the rearview mirror. And her timing could not have been better. Jake had already managed to wipe burger grease on the seat fabric and keep quiet about it, knowing Meghan wouldn't discover it until weeks later. From their back-seat views, Danny and Reece had seen the whole thing but had grown accustomed to Jake's pre-adolescent carelessness.

Having cruised these streets many times before, Meghan guided the group southbound on Route 91 toward Twinsburg, then Hudson, and would steer them to Cuyahoga Falls, all to the tunes of a Prince CD that belted from the stereo. A point of conflict since leaving the house, the musical choice was Meghan's personal favorite. Though the passengers had voiced their dissent, Meghan had quashed it with a my-car-my-rules response, much to their chagrin. Greg had adopted control of the volume switch and now turned the classic songs up a notch.

"Where are we headed?" Meghan shouted, her voice barely audible above the wind and Prince's crooning of "Little Red Corvette."

Jake leaned forward. "Let's go to a movie." He licked mustard from his fingers, then crumpled the burger wrapper and stuffed it into the map pocket behind the passenger seat.

"It's 11:30. The last shows have already started," Danny replied, confident their cruise would prolong until they settled for late-night pancakes at a Denny's restaurant.

"I could go for a shake, if you're up for it," shouted Jake. His comment earned a punch in the shoulder from Reece, who stared in disbelief.

"Man, you just got done eating. Why don't you digest it?"

"Here, take the rest of this." Danny shoved the remaining bites of a cheeseburger at his brother, who began stuffing his mouth without a second thought.

Reaching into his hip pocket, Danny found his pack of cigarettes and removed one. As he yanked a lighter from his other pocket, he poked the tar-and-nicotine stick into his mouth, then crouched down to escape the wind shear and light up. With the first inhale, he fell back in the seat, tightened his lips as he blew smoke toward the overcast sky. He watched as the plume of smoke whirled upon the wind and around the car.

Within seconds, Meghan shot her nose in the air. Her humming ceased, and Danny knew she'd detected the odor. She glared straight at Danny through the rearview mirror. Her head remained still, but her eyes could crack a rock.

"You know, that's so nasty. I hate when you smoke in my car."

With three feet of distance as a buffer between them, Danny grinned and blew a quick, haughty puff in her direction. Meghan clenched her jaw. Danny took this as a token reaction because he knew she thrived on attention from the Bale guys. She returned her attention to Prince, who now sang of driving to a place where someone's horses roam free.

Jake's head bolted forward. He exuded the type of sincerity

only a fourteen-year-old could muster with a sudden, naïve idea. "Hey Meg, can I drive?"

Meghan didn't even blink. "I'm sorry, did hell freeze over and someone forget to tell me?"

Their trek continued. Another minute passed before Reece finally verbalized the obvious: "Dude, we're like, roaming aimlessly around."

"I told you guys we should have left earlier," Greg said.

"And go where?"

"This isn't my town, man. Why don't you think of something?"

"I can think of a few things, but we can't take the *kids* along." Reece's claim, while an empty one, ignited a flame nonetheless, to which Danny provided a befitting retort with minimal effort. And so the traditional arguments began—spontaneous, brief, and good-natured—which always left the participants laughing in the end.

"All right," Meghan snapped. "Somebody decide where we're going, because I'm not gonna drive around all night."

Jake was on the ball. "I already offered a solution to that one."

Another pound in the arm from Reece. Meghan offered Jake a look of pity for the constant harassment, but she had grown up with the same shots from Greg and had managed to deal with it.

Drawing another puff, Danny flicked the ashes and rested his cigarette-laden hand on the car door. He relished these moments most. For all the pointless wandering and side arguments that erupted along the way, each Bale-Harting reunion arrived with eager anticipation on his part. In truth, Danny didn't care where they wound up or what would ensue that evening. He felt content right now. The way he saw it, the remaining hours constituted bonus time.

As he slouched in the back seat, Danny picked up the scent of Meghan's shampoo. And for no particular reason, he just looked at her as she stopped the CD and tuned to a Top 40 station, her head bobbing to Gin Blossoms. Danny watched as Greg spoke something to her and she turned to answer him. A streetlight raced by overhead and revealed a freckle on the back of her neck, a freckle Danny hadn't noticed before. Her puckered lips, her stubby chin, her delicate ears unveiled and hidden again by her hair in motion—Danny studied them all. More than any other person in the car, Danny savored Meghan's company. Her personality, razor sharp and a polar opposite to his own, captivated him. She could draw attention to herself with effortless flair. But in this late summer moment, a bittersweet delight emerged in Danny's heart. Like velvet purple incense, a nervous ache and a welcome pleasure. It ignited in Danny the desire to smile and shed a tear, both at the same time. Unable to reconcile this incongruity, he shook himself out of the emotional state and fed his lungs with more nicotine.

"Danny, you're quiet back there," Meghan called out.

"Oh, I was just thinking about something."

"Anything you'd like to share with the rest of the group?"

He had the sudden urge for a conversation with her, but his tongue grew lax in the unanticipated moment. Embarrassed, he began a desperate search for a topic of substance but wound up penniless. "Nope."

"You know, it's not polite to keep secrets. Didn't they teach you that in kindergarten?"

Feigning interest in the darkened roadside grass, Danny wouldn't risk eye contact. Instead, he peeped in her direction for

a split second, his eyebrows lifting in a mode that claimed innocence. "Tsk." Back to the darkened grass, praying for a change
in subject matter. One hint of detail and she would never let it
rest. He couldn't afford the humiliation, especially with Reece
sitting nearby consuming his fair share of oxygen. Granted,
at the moment, Reece seemed to pay him no attention, busy
joking around with Greg and terrorizing Jake. However, years
of experience had proven Reece's hearing impeccable.

After persevering a few moments, Danny proved victori-
ous as Meghan turned on the brights and focused on the road
ahead. She had veered and now approached a stretch of pave-
ment absent of traffic signals and intersections. And with the
passage of another mile, Meghan slumped back in her seat,
her usual indication that she'd reached the brink of boredom.
Interrupting the commotion, she glanced at the corner of the
back seat. "Hey Reece, switch places with me. I want to talk to
Danny."

"What, now?"

"Yeah. Hurry, before the traffic picks up."

"You're kind of busy with your foot on the pedal," Greg
chimed in.

"Take the wheel, Greg. And the pedal too."

Before he could object, her hands had abandoned the steering wheel, her knee already halfway up the backrest of the
driver's seat. Greg hurried to grab the wheel and forced his leg
over the middle partition, his eyes round with shock.

"What the hell, Meg! You're gonna get us all killed!"

"Just drive the car, Greg."

"Gee, what an idea!"

His options limited, Reece bolted to his feet and took a firm
grasp of Greg's headrest, as if he realized he'd better make it over

the seats first so *someone* would be behind the wheel. At Reece's reaction, Meghan waited a moment, then tried to squeeze past the two front seats anyway.

Reece, now stuck between both front seats and squirming to get loose, looked down to discover Meghan's head forcing its way through the open space between his legs. "Meghan, look out!" He jimmied a tad more.

Danny refused to blink and miss a single detail of the clown act. Once he'd figured his own death wasn't imminent, he found himself searching for routes out of the human maze as it unfolded before him.

Motionless, Greg shut his eyes. "Reece, get your ass out of my face."

"I can't help it! She's using up all the space! You could've done this an easier way, Meghan—maybe stop the car or something!"

Lunging forward with his life in his hands, Reece fumbled the wheel and landed on the driver's seat, at the mercy of gravity's tug. Still trying to maintain control of the circumstances, Meghan kicked her way out of her own predicament and, by accident, knocked Greg's hand off the steering wheel. The car took a violent swerve toward the shoulder of the road.

Greg gasped. "Reece, look out! There's a ditch right next to us!" he screamed like a girl.

Panicked, Reece gained control of the wheel and jerked the car back into the lane, pushing Meghan's leg away and sending her, head first, toward the back seat in a tumbled mess, her feet whipping through the air. At the sight of her midair, Danny took one last puff and flung his cigarette out of the car. Its ashes dispersed with a seething twinkle just before Meghan landed on Jake's lap. As Jake and Danny roared with laughter, Greg shook his head, his hand halfway over his eyes, trying to hide a smirk. Reece looked like he could sweat bullets as he inched, back and forth, against the seat, probably to determine whether he'd soiled himself in the process.

For all the adventure, Danny swore the car had only reached fifty miles an hour. An unusual feat, yet he was confident Meghan had survived riskier encounters in the past.

Meghan squeezed between the two youngest Bales and straightened her posture. And of course, her hair required fixing in the blowing wind.

"Well, that was easy," she said, adding in mockery, "Why don't you stop the car while we do this, Reece!"

"Shut up, Meghan." He'd continued to drive, so his pants must have been dry as talcum powder.

Not another word ensued as all five passengers grew calm, pulses and breathing patterns slowing to regularity. They reached the Cuyahoga Falls area, where a street lined with darkened retail windows told the group all was closed for the night. A handful of neon signs remained aglow but piqued no interest among the teenagers in the car.

Danny had all but forgotten about the car stereo, which persisted with The Cranberries' "Linger," oblivious to the recent excitement.

Without a sound, Danny peered over at Meghan, who had closed her eyes. She must have forgotten the conversation she'd deemed so crucial moments earlier. Even Jake had managed to doze. Danny could overhear Greg telling Reece about his upcoming college journey.

And once again, Danny picked up the trace of Meghan's shampoo. Self-conscious, he elevated his knees higher as he sunk further in his seat, overcome with keen awareness of his surroundings and the subtle movements of all who filled them.

He found himself intrigued by the older girl seated beside him—the girl with whom he had been acquainted his entire life, but about whom, in practicality, he knew very little. Danny wondered what it was like to spend Tuesdays with her.

As if she could read his train of thought, Meghan opened her eyes and sunk down into her seat until their faces were cheek to cheek. The car rolled down an incline, and she crossed her arms as a chill in the air sent goose-bumps over them.

Danny's stomach quivered again. He sought something— anything—to break the silence. "When do you start school?" he asked.

"Next week," she replied. "Senior year, so it should fly. I can't wait to get out."

"Me too. I've got a while to go, though. You looking at colleges?"

"My dad keeps pushing me on it, but I can't stand the thought of being chained down for another four years."

She tacked on a halfhearted pout, as if she couldn't care less for sympathy but offered the expression anyway. Her eyes, crystal blue and illumined by passing streetlights, appeared deeper than Danny remembered them. They seemed to speak volumes, as if to invite him to look into the depths of her soul.

His nervousness ached more.

"My boyfriend might go to Ball State to play basketball," Meghan continued. "He's so talented. They really want him."

"How long have you two been going out?"

"Since January." She slapped her knee. "I should've brought our junior prom picture to show you. Oh, well." She gave Danny a gentle nudge. "So now that you know all my personal details, is there a hot babe in *your* life, Danny Boy?"

He shrugged. "There's a girl who rode my bus last year,

kinda good looking. We talked a lot during the ride home. I may ask her out."

"Hmm." Meghan nodded, a smirk at the corner of her mouth. "You play hard to get, don't you, Dan the Man!" She poked at his ribs.

Danny squirmed, attempted to maintain a straight face, playfully twisted in his seat until she ceased her platonic attack.

As she twirled a lock of hair with her finger, Danny stared straight ahead and replayed mental pictures of the tease that had ended far too soon. Mustering soft courage, he turned to her and broke the stillness.

"I would've taken you to your prom if your boyfriend couldn't," he whispered. "Would you have gone with me?"

Another moment lingered, then Meghan turned her face toward his. With nary a movement, she leaned her head toward him, a knowing gleam in her eye.

"Yeah, I would've." And with that, as smoothly as she had leaned in his direction, Meghan resumed her position as if nothing had occurred.

His heartbeat on a gradual rise, Danny responded with a nod of coolness, his cheeks growing hot. Cocking his head toward the side of the road, he fought to hide his contented smile.

CHAPTER 4
MAY 2007

At the edge of the street, Danny climbed out of his gray Chevy to empty his mailbox. Arriving home well past midnight, he had stayed to clean the kitchen at McGrady's after a Tuesday late shift. In an attempt to catch a preview of his mail by moonlight, he held a couple of letters at an angle but couldn't decipher any characters.

Pulling up the gravel driveway, Danny parked beneath the carport and turned off the engine. Tired, his face pasted with sweat and clothes covered with grease stains, he plodded to the house's side door. The lock, in dire need of lubrication, had stuck for months, a task he'd vowed to accomplish at an abstract future date. In the meantime, a strategic jiggle forced its compliance. He hauled his feet through the door, flipped on the light, and tossed the mail on the kitchen table.

Danny lived alone.

The single-story house, built decades before tourists had discovered the area, was a standing relic at Sunset Beach. A few blocks from a trailer park and tucked away to the convenience of the local municipality, it resided at the outskirts of town, sheltered—or perhaps hidden—from the pastel commercialization of the city's main boulevard. Surrounded by sparse, thirsty land-scaping, the house's whitewashed siding exhibited a shameless admission of its age, a reminder of what Sunset Beach had once been: a southern, post-Civil War town, population four hundred, founded by an even smaller group of freed slaves. Given the rapid expansion over the last ten years, Danny had no doubt the house would fall victim to a bulldozer one day. But in the meantime, it remained a structural war-horse, unseen by the thousands of visitors who entered and left the city.

Danny rented the house from a sweet retired lady named Doris, who had moved to the beach with her husband in the 1970s. Frequent seasonal customers at McGrady's, Danny had acquainted himself with her relatives through countless chit-chats when they came to visit Grandma and Gramps at the beach. After a few years of widowhood, Doris had sought an even warmer climate and moved in with her son's family in Flagstaff, Arizona. Prior to her departure, she and Danny had arrived at a lax lease agreement. Today, he could picture the lively woman, thrilled with the idea of opening her mailbox to find a rent check awaiting, tearing the recurrent envelopes open like a child untying a ribbon from a birthday gift. Doris had told him she loved the idea of having the house occupied by a young resident, just the way she remembers it. A good thing for Danny; were her son to invest some money to update the house, Doris could earn a larger profit marketing it as a frugal alternative to the otherwise expensive Sunset Beach vacation rentals.

Shaking his head at such a notion, Danny wandered to the living room, his favorite room in the house: Yellowed blinds. Hardwood floors aged to perfection. Second-hand furniture Danny had purchased at various garage sales. A pale afghan arrayed a wine-colored sofa, and the old armchair beside it reminded him of an Agatha Christie novel. In one corner sat a television and stereo, nestled between a bookcase and a brown brick fireplace. Comfortable yet dim, the room possessed an overall grandparent feel.

Ripping off his socks and changing into a pair of shorts, Danny jogged to the other side of the room and grabbed his guitar, which had leaned against the sofa all day, untouched. He refused to climb into bed before making an effort to write. A nightly ritual, he endeavored to pour his emotions like fuel into the art he loved. Despite the fact that, for no apparent reason, his productivity level varied with each attempt, Danny had committed himself to improving his craft.

With the guitar in one hand and mail in the other, he slid out the back door to the patio, where he turned on the porch light. He set the mail on a small, round table. Danny crawled into a plastic chair and sat cross-legged, guitar in his lap. With the pluck of some strings, he determined the instrument required tuning and adjusted it on the fly. Then he resumed his strumming.

At the moment, he had no subject ideas for a song—the most typical hurdle he confronted and the most difficult to overcome. Taking a creative stab, he formed some words over a chord, trying to locate hidden treasure.

"Mmm, your eyes are dancing flames," he sang. A decent start; it could have been worse. "Mmm, your eyes, they dance before me like fire ..."

He stopped. Something, perhaps the chord, didn't sound accurate. Realigning his fingers, he shifted to a new key.

"Like a flame to wax, you melt my heart with your gentle stare." Satisfied with the new chord, he progressed to the next.

"And anytime you shed a tear, call my name and I'll be there."
Borderline cliched, but it had potential. "And baby, I ..." Danny
frowned, searching for the next phrase. "Baby, I ..." He leaned
his head forward with anticipation, but his focus ran dry. His
voice softening to a whisper, Danny curled his lip and plucked
each individual note in the trio. "Baby, I ..."

Distracted, he yielded to a mindless feat of spontaneity,
strumming a feverish chord progression like a Mexican story-
book hero serenading a captivated *seniorita*. After that, with a
crooked grin, Danny mastered the first line of "My Dog Has
Fleas" before he ceased playing. Faced with a mental block, he
felt too exhausted to navigate an escape.

Rubbing his eyes, Danny laid the guitar on the ground and
took a deep breath, puffed his cheeks and let out a prolonged
exhale. He dragged the miniature table in front of him and
rested his feet on top, then degenerated into an empty stare.
Leaning back in the wobbly chair, he locked his hands behind
his head and let his body go limp.

Danny listened.

No human voices. Seagulls had disappeared for the night.
The patio made direct contact with a small stretch of beach,
where limestone-colored sand had beckoned Danny forward on
a regular basis during his tenure at the House of Doris. Oftentimes he imagined the frisky lady in a former era, fighting to
take a morning run atop the radiated grains, her husband fighting to keep up with her.

As Danny ingested the sound of the ocean, he allowed its
tossing waves to seep three-dimensionally into his ears. Salty
air invigorated his senses and left a misty residue on his face.
Breathing amid summer humidity felt like sucking oven air
through a straw, but Danny's lungs thrived on this brand of

oxygen most.

In the evenings, Danny would gaze at the horizon that expanded before him like open arms. Devoid of neighbors, his back door ushered him to a fresh world of creativity where water met sky. He would watch red and sherbet-orange sunsets fall with tender grace on the emerald water, waves dancing before him in shimmering beauty. Along the shoreline, the sand was flat and compact, glazed over by small breakers that rubbed across it in a steady caress. Closer to his patio, fragments of driftwood had ridden ashore with the morning tide.

To the dismay of his parents, Danny moved to Sunset Beach at the age of twenty-four. Prior to that, he attended the University of North Carolina—Charlotte where, between homework and obligations to the campus business fraternity, he honed his songwriting craft on evenings and weekends.

During those college years, Danny visited countless coffee shops, immersing himself in the retro ambience. With years of amateur writing already under his belt, he sought opportunities to hear local singer-songwriters. Open-mic nights highlighted an array of talent ranging from hippie folk singers to jazz-rap experimentalists, all pouring their hearts forth like a river. Danny simply listened, a witness to the live, enigmatic connection that seemed to emerge between performer and audience. Unduplicated and unrivaled by compact disc, he found the phenomenon intriguing. Danny never desired to become a celebrity. Instead, he followed suit with these coffeehouse singers, entertaining a modest group of listeners and reaping immediate results.

He didn't craft songs for commercial sales. He yearned to ignite a live audience.

Eager to bid farewell to academia, Danny graduated with

a master's degree in Finance and an emphasis on real estate. A solid field and a safe career route, he judged. Besides, business classes had held his interest to an adequate extent. His academic accomplishment pleased his corporate-lawyer father, and, when he allowed himself to admit it, Danny felt satisfied that a four-year portion of his life had wound up fruitful.

Upon departing college, Danny secured his first job at a lending firm in downtown Cleveland, a salaried position in the home mortgage division on the ninth floor of the office tower, where he spent many evenings working unpaid over-time. During his lunch hour, when the mild summer weather appeared, he would purchase a meatball sandwich and sit in front of Lake Erie a few blocks away.

But the northern Ohio winters nearly deadened him, or so it felt, as he peered out the window at impatient traffic that bus-tled along slushy, snow-bordered streets beneath an ashen sky. So after a couple of years of white-collar routine, Danny, sick of massaging numbers, decided he needed to leave. He wanted to write, and he couldn't do so with frozen fingers or stiff wrists. Pinpointing an apartment on the Internet, Danny loaded his car to capacity and risked relocation to Sunset Beach without a job and without acquaintances.

His parents questioned the abruptness of his decision. Danny, however, was not surprised. He had sensed an internal friction build at a steady rate, and combustion was imminent, though he'd expected it to manifest decades later in the form of a midlife crisis.

Tonight, Danny leaned forward in the patio chair, lit a ciga-rette and gazed down the shoreline. In the distance, a multitude of lights speckled through numerous hotel and condominium windows. With a smug laugh, he estimated how much money visitors spent on lodging, restaurants and flashy souvenir shops in any given week. By his calculation, they burned more cash than it cost him to live there.

Danny's stream of consciousness now took a sudden detour. His mind turned to Meghan Harting, which was not uncommon. He wondered about her often: Had she found contentment? Was she married or single? Was she curious about him as well?

All through his college stint, he had kept close in touch with Meghan on a weekly basis, always through snail-mail letters. Meghan believed email hid personal traits identifiable through nuances in handwriting—its twists, slants, pressure points, and for Meghan, those triple underlines. But after several years, her romantic involvement with Brian accelerated, which left her friendship with Danny in neglect. Longer periods passed between letters until her next one never arrived. In an attempt to rekindle their communication, Danny had written to Meghan's last known address after his move to the beach.

She'd never responded.

Danny stifled a yawn, reached for the stack of mail and sorted through the junk. The last item was a letter from his brother, Reece, who wanted to hang out with him at the beach during an upcoming military leave. Thrilled with the news, Danny sat up straight. He had seen his brother on rare occasion since their teens. By skipping college to enlist in the armed forces as soon as possible, Reece had fulfilled a childhood dream. After years invested in overseas deployment, Reece now lived on a base in Kentucky, where he trained other service members.

Danny folded the letter and returned it to its envelope.

As Danny sat beneath a blackened sky, a peculiar fact plagued him: Despite living here in a personal paradise, emptiness had settled within him. Unable to reconcile the disparity, it had pricked at Danny for several months now.

Extinguishing his cigarette, Danny picked up his guitar and the remaining mail, then headed inside for the night. Jay hadn't scheduled him to work the next day. Danny was ready to crash until ten.

CHAPTER 5
OCTOBER 1995

Hordes of Saturday shoppers filled the suburban shopping mall. As he wandered with Meghan through a department store in the east wing, Danny shook his head at how much earlier the stores seemed to unleash their Christmas decorations each year. Autumn had begun just a few weeks ago, yet he and Meghan walked past a barrage of flashing lights and plastic ornaments. In the air, Danny picked up the aroma of artificial pine trees, each tree sprayed with room-temperature snow, aerosol-scented and fresh from an Arizona factory. But in spite of the store's blatant attempt to enhance its year-end bottom line, shoppers did not appear stricken with festive fever, judging from the scarcity of shopping bags they carried around.

Meghan brushed her hand along a pricey black purse, then continued to browse. Danny followed two steps behind. He found the scenario humorous, watching nineteen-year-old Meghan give serious consideration to items she would never actually use. With one credit card in her purse, its application cosigned by her parents, she and Danny considered the possibilities of a five-hundred-dollar credit limit endless.

Meghan picked up a pair of black high heels and dangled

them on her finger by the straps. "Would you say I'm a high-heeled kind of girl?"

Danny shook his head without pretending to care. Crumpling her lips, Meghan returned the shoes to their display pedestal, then shifted her focus to her true scavenger hunt.

"I need you to help me find a birthday present for my boyfriend. That's really why I dragged you in here."

Relieved, Danny led the way to the escalator. They ascended to the second floor to continue their quest in the men's department.

With retail options at a minimum in Oxford, the two teenagers had abandoned the rest of their clans for an afternoon in nearby Cincinnati. Danny despised malls and secretly hoped to cross paths with a complimentary demo of a massage chair. But Meghan needed quality male input. If forced to rely on his brother Jake's advice, Danny knew she would settle for a pair of glow-in-the-dark boxers to shut Jake up, followed by a trip to return those boxers the next weekend.

Reaching the end of their ride, Danny and Meghan stepped off of the escalator, ignoring another plastic tree on their way to the cotton sweaters. Meghan pointed to a mannequin covered in a harvest-orange Henley. "What about that?" she asked.

"It's pretty standard; I'd wear it. Different color—brown, maybe. What size is he?"

"A little taller than you. Grab a large."

Hunched over, Danny sifted through the assortment of sizes until he located the size. He handed the sweater to Meghan, who unfolded it and held it against Danny's chest.

"Is it gonna work out?" asked Danny.

"I can't tell while you're slouching."

When he straightened up, Meghan readjusted the sweater

and stood back as far as her arms would allow. She scanned the sweater against him, up and down, until her eyes landed at the bottom.

"I think we'd better go with the tall version."

Danny crouched down and grabbed the article on top of the stack, which another customer had obviously sampled and refolded in a failed attempt at helpfulness. Before he had a chance to straighten his knees, Meghan pointed at the sweater.

"Hey, could you please grab a different one? It gives me the creeps to think who might've tried that thing on last," she said.

"Are you kidding?"

"No."

"Would you like me to remove that pea from underneath your mattress while I'm at it?"

Meghan smacked him in playful retaliation. "I worked in a clothing store in high school. One time, a guy came in, tried on a bunch of stuff. He was so disgusting, sweating all over the place—and smelled like a toilet." Her hand raised as though to enhance the validity of the claim, she shook the willies from her shoulder and turned her eyes back to the sweater display.

"Are you sure that kind of guy doesn't turn you on?"

"I sprayed the fitting room with disinfectant after he left."

"Geez," Danny ridiculed. "Fine, I'll humor you. Life's too short." He found another large-tall and handed it to her as she started toward the cashier.

"Thank you."

"Whatever."

Meghan whipped out her credit card to pay for the purchase, which would leave the majority of her five-hundred-dollar limit intact. Danny knew Meghan cared less about the card's credit limit and more about its snazzy photo of a hot air balloon.

Bag in hand, they walked out of the store and into the mall corridor. Eyeing a pet store window, Meghan darted toward a litter of overpriced beagles. "Oh, how cute!"

Danny ran to catch up with her. Together they watched as one of the puppies tripped over its ears and landed against its brother.

"If you had a puppy, what would you name it?" Meghan asked.

"Richard."

Meghan chuckled, then moved to the next window, where one Chihuahua drifted into a cozy nap inside its food bowl. Another puppy poked its way around the bowl's perimeter to snatch a morsel from under its sleeping sibling.

"Where are you working now?" Danny asked.

"At a local accounting office. Receptionist."

"So you're learning the secrets of the trade?"

"I just transfer the calls and greet the people who come in." Meghan tapped on the window to distract one of the animals, but they ignored her, fearless behind the glass barrier. "It pays the bills. Plus, they'll do my taxes for free." Losing interest in pet prospects, she continued to window-shop next door, Danny at her side. Meghan added, "I've gotta say, I don't miss high school at all, the cliques and hall passes."

Danny nodded in agreement. "I can't wait to get out. I've started checking out colleges."

"Like where?"

"My folks and I visited Ohio State a while back. I also got some info on University of North Carolina."

"Why North Carolina?"

"I had relatives who lived there for a couple of years, so we used to visit them. I loved it, especially when we went to the coast for the weekend. So having the beach a few hours away from college would be an added bonus."

"The foundation of a quality education! I'm proud of ya."

"Hey, I'll probably apply to Kent State too, just to keep that option open since it's close to home. But I do want to go away to school."

A costume-jewelry boutique caught Meghan's attention next, beckoned her to a silver earring display. Danny cringed but followed her inside the store anyway.

"Does your girlfriend want you to stay in town?"

Danny shrugged. "We haven't talked a lot about it, but it's a given that we're gonna part ways. She wants to go to Yale and major in sociology."

"So she's pretty smart, huh?"

"That's an understatement. She's trying to decide if she should keep taking her honors calculus class next semester or just settle for the regular version. Blows me away."

"You deserve a smart girl, kiddo."

As Meghan lavished him with a side hug and a vigorous rub on the back, Danny felt the glow of daybreak in his chest.

"Are the two of you pretty serious?" Meghan asked.

In an effort to distract Meghan from probing further, Danny held a pumpkin necklace to her neck in jest.

Laughing, she said, "Oh sure—if I was twelve!" Seizing the trinket, she returned it to the display but demoted it to the bottom of the rack. "You never answered my question: Are you two serious?"

He tried to gloss over his half-hearted response with an enthusiastic tone. "She's cool. Cute, too."

"But something's missing?"

"I didn't say that."

"You're transparent. I've known you way too long."

"Ah, don't make a big deal about it. We're fine. I mean, it's not like I'm obligated to marry her." Danny glanced at his watch. "Want to get something to drink?"

• • •

A sea of circus décor engulfed three sections of tables in the mall food court. They claimed an open table in the center section. Parched, Danny wasted no time with his cherry cola. Meghan dug her way into a dish of low-fat frozen yogurt, though Danny saw no need for her to monitor her weight. As he eased back in his chair, he studied the people around them, a habit more than a curiosity.

Meghan perked up. "All right, Danny Boy. If you could go anywhere, do anything with your life, what would it be?"

He narrowed his eyes and wondered if her motives were less than innocent, but decided to take his chances and wade in. "How big are you talking?"

"Doesn't matter. It's a dream." With a gung-ho thrust of the fist, she added, "Set your expectations high, young man, and you will rise to the occasion."

Danny didn't hesitate with his answer. "I would write. I'd hole up in my own office and let the songs flow. And since this is a dream, there's no business side to it, so I'd tinker around with different time signatures that you couldn't dance to, just to see where it takes me. I'd release a bunch of CDs that have artistic covers, like those album covers from the '70s." He leaned forward. "I don't care much about getting famous from them. Plus, I'd develop other artists and write for them. That way, even if there *was* a business side and it reached the point where my CDs were no longer trendy, I could still earn a living as a writer for the up-and-comers." Danny paused, then added with a wink, "Oh, and I'd also own a jet."

Meghan nodded. She cocked her head and gazed at him as if he were an oversized eyeball in a Picasso painting. From the way she raised an eyebrow, you would think she'd acquired a piece of blackmail material. She took another bite of her raspberry yogurt.

"What about you?" Danny asked.

Meghan swallowed. Squinting, she hummed in monotone to herself, then said, "I'd definitely live on the shore. And it would have to be tropical. None of that cold Cape Cod stuff." As she spoke, Danny felt his muscles go limp at the idea of hot sand and water that looked like liquid sapphire.

Meghan continued, "A Caribbean island with a resort for people to flock to, but otherwise deserted. I'd live a few miles from work, far enough to get away from the walkers. My own private stretch of beach as far as the eye can see."

Her eyes sparkled with delight. Danny could taste the saltwater and feel a healthy tan tingle on his skin.

"Where would you work?" he asked.

"I'd want to show people a good time, so an activity director at a resort would be right up my alley. There's a side of responsibility to it, but you're not tied to your desk—you can walk around, mingle with the people, get to know visitors from all over the world. Like Julie what's-her-name on *The Love Boat*. Then, when the workday ends, I'd head over to my house—"

"You mean your straw hut?"

"A two-story house with a view."

"Sounds expensive."

She shot him a look. "High expectations, remember?"

Danny crossed his arms and settled back in his chair as Meghan unveiled more.

"As I was saying, in the evenings, I would head home—to the house I can afford because I'd earn a salary large enough to pay for it in full." Danny rolled his eyes, but she ignored him. "When I got there, I'd borrow a recipe from the resort chefs to cook a little island cuisine. Then, my husband would arrive home from work. The love of my life—a *good* guy, not a jerk. He would treat me with respect, and he'd be a romantic. We'd eat dinner on the deck, sipping red wine and gazing out at the ocean. Then maybe on Saturdays, we'd make love on the shore, behind our house."

"In the open daylight?"

"On a remote corner of the island, remember?"

"That's right, in back of your straw hut."

"Shut up. This is *my* dream." She reached across and jiggled his arm. "Besides, we agreed this didn't need to be realistic."

"Good thing for that." Danny grinned.

CHAPTER 6
MAY 2007

Shutting the door behind her, Meghan could hear the roar of sports fans coming from the den as Brian watched a baseball game on the sofa. A half-empty beer bottle rested on the coffee table beside a thick, unlit candle, surrounded by paperwork and art samples. The sight had grown more frequent in recent months. While he often left the office early to beat Cincinnati's downtown traffic, Meghan knew Brian was among the first to arrive at the building each morning and had developed the gradual habit of taking work home with him. Meghan suspected he also perused paperwork during his highway commutes, though she had never asked him.

Approaching from behind, she wrapped her arms around his neck and leaned forward with a kiss. Without removing his eyes from the sea of white sheets, Brian tilted his chin upward in a token gesture of acknowledgement. His visage reflected the wear and tear of a solid day's work, the physical indication of hours spent staring at similar papers and skipping lunch along the way. Dressed down in a golf shirt and a pair of khaki Dockers, Brian appeared to have arrived home exhausted, wanting simply to grab a drink and grow numb for the evening. And in his typical fashion, he'd refused to indulge in such a luxury.

"How was school?" he asked.

"Fine. Last exam is finally over," she replied on the way to the bedroom to deposit her purse and shoes. Raising her voice from that distance, she continued, "I ran into my dad while I was there, so we got chili for lunch uptown."

Brian offered a hum of approval. He reached for his beer bottle as a baseball bat cracked and a runner advanced to third.

When she returned to the living room, Meghan wound her hair into a ponytail as she sat down beside her boyfriend and put her hand on his thigh. "Who's winning?"

"We are, if Avery gets the next run batted in."

Another crack of the bat prompted a collective cheer among the crowd, followed by a collective groan. Avery was safe, but the catcher had tagged the runner at home plate.

Brian grunted, shaking his head as he gulped a swig of honey brown. "Avery ..."

Meghan's interest in the game had begun to wane already. She ran her fingers through his hair. "Are you tired?"

With a prolonged blink of the eyes, he nodded. "It was non-stop today. My boss called me into his office first thing this morning, one-on-one. Said it was urgent."

"Is there anything wrong?"

Brian came to life. His eyebrows lifted, and he turned toward Meghan as the third inning concluded. "Actually, it was good news. His promotion is a done deal. Announced it today. They're moving him to corporate headquarters in New York."

"He needed an individual meeting to tell you that?"

Brian circled his finger along the ring of the bottleneck. "He also said he's got me lined up for a promotion."

Meghan squealed. She shook his knee with her hand,

crawled forward to kiss him. He dropped his poker face and a smile emerged. Meghan snuggled against him and went limp. "Brian, that's wonderful!"

Both hands still on the paper trail, Brian eyed the television as the top of the fourth inning began. "My job's in New York, too. He's creating a position right under him."

Meghan pushed back, her mouth wide open. "What? When do you need to give him an answer?"

"I already told him we'd be there. The job won't be ready for me until January, though."

"*We?* Wait, this is the first I've heard about it."

"It's not like you have a job that's keeping you here. Not a career one, anyway. This'll be good for both of us. Why *wouldn't* you want to go? You've told me countless times how you'd love to see New York."

"Seeing it and living there are two different things. Brian, our families live around here. And why didn't you run this past me before committing me to a lifestyle change?"

"Honey, why are you so offended? There are plenty of apartment offices up there, if that's what you're concerned about," he jeered.

"Don't you think I should have some input on this?"

"Meg, you don't know anything about the advertising industry. It's a fast-paced field. I need to seize this opportunity while I can."

"So you went behind my back, gave your approval, and decided you'd carry me along like a doll?" At Brian's vacant stare, Meghan added, "Is this for us, or is it for *you?*"

"Of course it's for us! What is it you don't like about this promotion?"

"It's not the promotion, Brian. It's the fact that you don't trust me to be a full part of your life!"

Brian halted. Now he dropped his paperwork and glared at her. Meghan watched his facial muscles constrict as he clenched his jaw.

"What are you talking about?" he shouted, thrusting his hands in front of him. "How don't I trust you?"

"Oh, please! Like you don't already know! I mean, you even went and bought this *house* by yourself. You didn't bother to tell me about it until after the closing!"

"I didn't want to distract you with the details."

"Well, maybe I wanted to contribute half of the down payment, half of the mortgage—something!"

Brian chuckled. "You mean with your big bucks from Oxford Meadows? Come on, this house cost more than a few paychecks, Meg!"

"I was content with our apartment in the first place! I only wanted to be with you. I couldn't have cared less how many rooms the place has!"

Brian shot up from the sofa. "Look, what does it matter? I thought we should have a nice house, and I didn't want to bog you down with the payments. What's the crime in that?"

"That's sweet, but I don't need you to make decisions on my behalf, like I have no control over my life and need you to supply for me!"

"This is our home—together!"

Meghan felt her lips tighten. "No, Brian, this is *your* home. I'm just the guest who shares the bedroom with an advertising executive. You make me feel like a prostitute!"

"You're being ridiculous. I just think I'm more qualified to make those decisions for us, that's all."

"What are you saying?"

"Simply put, it takes a bit more prowess to succeed in advertising than in a leasing office. The facts speak for themselves."

"That's so arrogant!"

"But it pays the bills, right?" His stare turned to granite.

Meghan hurt inside. And even now, as she shouted, she noticed Brian stood above her, physically looking down upon her like he would a child. She darted up to her feet so she could pierce his eyes with hers.

"Don't you realize by now that I don't care about your money?" she said. "Don't you know me better than that after eight years?"

Brian's complexion turned a deeper shade of pink. "Look, I want this career, and I'm not giving it up, so deal with it!"

He didn't just say that, did he? she thought.

Meghan took half a step back and crossed her arms. "Why do you even want me around? So you'll have a date for your business functions? So everyone can see how well you've ironed out your life? 'Look at Brian! Man, he's so stable—solid career, a woman that adores him. What a sharp guy he is!' Is that it? You need someone to drape all over you when it's convenient and public? I'm not a wind-up toy!"

"You didn't have a problem with that stuff before."

"I didn't realize it would be permanent!"

"Meghan, that's part of the game."

"Well, I'm not your trophy." Meghan turned her back and stormed into the kitchen. She heard Brian pounce back onto the sofa and shuffle his papers. Still breathing fire and unable to focus, probably.

Meghan yanked a frozen entrée from the freezer and slammed it into the microwave. Grabbing a can of green beans, she assaulted it with a can opener and dumped the vegetables into a bowl in a careless heap.

Similar tension had mounted between Meghan and Brian for years, such that Meghan now took these battles with stride. But she could sense the weight of the consequential toll. Its friction grated on her heart and left emotional rug burns. While able to release each day's arguments, Meghan had spent count-less nights in mental labor over the relationship itself, drifting to sleep unsettled and without answers.

After she heated a frozen meatloaf in the microwave and transferred it to a large dish, Meghan felt a pair of hands on her arms and a head rest upon her shoulder. A gentle massage fol-lowed, then a familiar phrase: "I'm sorry."

The words sounded so worn coming from Brian's mouth. Over time, the phrase had lost its healing sparkle. In the past, Meghan would have softened toward reconciliation. Nowadays, at the sound of this all-too-familiar apology, Meghan felt her stomach muscles contract, tight with stress.

"I'm tired of hearing that all the time." She kept her voice calm, but only because she felt deflated inside.

"I know. Look," Brian said, turning her delicate body to bring her eyes to his. "I want to make this relationship succeed. Whatever it takes, I'm going to make the effort. Things will change."

Flinching, Meghan responded, "Do you realize what you're saying?"

"How can you ask that? What can I do to make you feel better?"

Meghan bit her lip, aching and angry that, after their long-term relationship, Brian remained content to consider her a stranger to his heart.

"I want you to love me," she replied.

Brian drew her near, wrapped his arms around her.
Yet Meghan found the habitual embrace disturbing.
It was lifeless. Shallow.
Empty.

CHAPTER 7
JUNE 2007

With four bottles of beer balanced in his grip, Jay McGrady edged his way between crowded tables. Lava Lamp Bar could hardly accommodate its own chairs and barstools, much less the people who occupied them. Through crackling speakers, Axl Rose hollered "Welcome to the Jungle" over a wailing guitar. A hideaway for the locals and an eyesore at Sunset Beach, tourists neither had a clue how to find the tiny bar, nor would they ruin their paradise vacation by stepping foot inside.

Danny and the rest of Jay's group had shoved two mismatched tables together, added an extra ashtray, and spent the last hour contributing plumes of gray cigarette smoke to the already hazy room.

"Here we are, kids!" shouted Jay when he reached the group. By default, Jay became the self-appointed entertainer at any gathering due to the fact that, without exception, his voice boomed loudest. Taking his seat at one end, Jay rubbed a spot on the filthy table and wiped the mystery substance against a chipped, wooden edge.

Wednesday nights at Lava Lamp were a tradition for Danny, Jay and about seven others, most of them McGrady's employees.

After a year sharing rounds of drinks at McGrady's, Jay decided to change their location so he could spy out his restaurant's seedier competition.

"McGrady, I think you finished half the bottles that are sitting here," a co-worker shouted from halfway down the table.

"Ah, they wouldn't let me suck the tap, man!"

It was a well-known fact that Jay could hold more liquor than any other person at the table, a result of sneaking behind the McGrady's kitchen and nursing his tolerance between tasks.

Tonight, seated at the table's far end, Danny retreated even further from his friends as he scribbled on a pocket notepad. He tried to ignore the faint scent of aged hot dogs, thawed and cooked at one corner of the bar. Danny grew absorbed in his creative exercise as he strained for potential song titles, a practice he'd perfected on fast-food napkins as a teenager. Lounging beside him was Shannon, an informal blind date courtesy of Jay, who had decided Danny's love life warranted a respirator. Jay had spotted Shannon earlier that afternoon as she exited a nail salon and had, in his own inexplicable way, deemed Shannon's personality compatible with Danny's.

Jay was wrong.

However, Danny was pleased to discover that, after rattling at the mouth and vying for Jay's status as entertainment champion, Shannon grew less verbal with a few margaritas drifting through her veins.

The blond beauty had fawned over Danny all evening. Yet after her innumerable attempts to captivate her new beau with flashy smiles and frequent eye contact, Danny's taste for the overbearing woman had peaked within their first ten minutes together. Nonetheless, during a dart game a few minutes ago, he had promised Jay not to leave the girl stranded for the evening.

A request more selfish than considerate, as even Jay had begun to question his own matchmaking skills as he listened to Shannon's rapid chatter all evening. In fact, her margaritas were Jay's idea—to booze her up and calm her down.

Over the course of the evening, sporadic bursts of laughter had erupted from individuals around the table. Shannon had teased Danny with pokes to the belly, to which he'd offered a perfunctory smile to placate her. Yet, in spite of his patronizing responses, it seemed Shannon had deluded herself into believing Danny had become enthralled with her.

For Danny, the minutes seemed to drudge forward in thirty-second intervals. What he wouldn't have given to be somewhere else at this moment.

And with that, a new title appeared on his notepad: "Get Me Out of Here."

At last, Shannon peered over his shoulder, mouthed syllables in a vain attempt to decipher his illegible handwriting. "You taking notes or something?"

Caught off guard, Danny ceased his brainstorm and closed the notepad. How many minutes had he ignored her? He'd lost track.

Danny feigned innocence. "Oops, sorry about that," he said.

Tongue lodged against her cheek, Shannon perked up, as if thrilled to have his full attention. Danny felt sorry for her.

"He's always working on something," Jay shouted with alcohol-induced candor. "The guy's relentless. But the ladies dig his stuff."

Shannon leaned closer to Danny, the corner of her mouth upturned. "Really ..." Her eyelids met halfway as she scrutinized Danny's eyes. "Hmm ..."

Jay continued to ramble, pointing at her with the neck of his

Budweiser bottle. "You should stop by the restaurant and hear him. Fridays and Saturdays, baby."

"So he's a good singer, huh?"

"Hey, all I can say is—and this is *not* just the liquor talking—business has gone up since I let him take the stage. I discovered him, you know." He winked at Danny. "That would make you my protégé, wouldn't it, Danny Boy?"

Danny nearly choked on a gulp of beer as he downplayed a chuckle. *Protégé* must have two definitions. Apparently that liquor had acquired a voice—and had begun to compose its own dictionary in the process.

Shannon examined Danny further.

• • •

Americana lampposts, their sculpted metal columns painted hunter green, lined the sidewalks of The Landing. One by one, employees unplugged neon store signs as closing time arrived. Aiming for the parking lot, customers carried their final purchases in brown bags, tossing empty beverage cups and ice cream dishes into retro trashcans along the way.

Wandering from a section of small carnival rides at the eastern end of The Landing, Danny and Shannon wove through sidewalks alongside lingering tourists, many of whom held hands during a romantic interlude. As if determined to label the date a success, Shannon had suggested she and Danny meet at The Landing for a carousel ride after the bar. Though reluctant, Danny had agreed. In an effort to spare her feelings, he concealed any manifestation of boredom and reminded himself that this date would end in due time.

The Landing personified nostalgia: A saltwater taffy store

with a *Buy 1 Box, Get 1 Free* sign taped to its door. A porcelain doll boutique, its windows arrayed with toddler-sized human replicas. A bookshop outfitted like a 1920s New York City newsstand.

As Danny and Shannon strolled down the sidewalk, the passerby population thinned in size around them. The pitter-patter of flip-flop footwear faded by the minute.

"I love summer," Shannon said in a clear attempt to resuscitate the moment.

Hands in his pockets, Danny pursed his lips. From his peripheral vision, he watched Shannon study his profile. No doubt, Shannon was savvy enough to realize his mind had been in motion all evening, despite his silence. And without looking at her, Danny could tell she was on a search for the combination that would unlock his mouth.

"You're one of those quiet types," she said at last.

Danny nodded in reply. Perhaps his silence was borderline rude. Shannon wasn't a bad person, and his frustration in life wasn't her fault. What harm could a little conversation do?

"Where do you work, Shannon?"

"At a jewelry store a few miles away."

"So you sell engagement rings, things like that?"

"Actually, it's tourist jewelry. Shells, beads, that kind of thing."

"Sorry, my mistake."

More silence. But the mood felt lighter already.

Shannon furled her eyebrows before she spoke again. "Can I ask you something?"

"Sure." Now he was curious. If she'd asked for permission, her next question was bound to be a gem.

"How does a silent guy like you get in front of an audience

and sing?"

He was impressed with her observation. Indeed, he had asked himself the same question many times before but had never found a suitable answer.

"Hard to say," he replied. "The best way I can describe it is, I come alive when I'm behind a microphone. It's like I reach down into this deep part of myself and become the person I was created to be. That's difficult to do when I'm not performing."

"Why do you think that is?"

Danny gave her a broad smile. "Music's my passion. There are certain things expressed with songs that can't be communicated any other way because the music enhances the words. The musical notes—the way they interact and layer upon each other—make the lyrics richer." Danny could sense life returning to his eyes as he tried to clothe the abstract. "In fact, there are times when I can't express a feeling with words, but a chord will state it clearly."

They continued to wander along. Shannon's shoulders had an easygoing sway as she walked, an effortless flair that spoke of contentment in life.

"How long have you lived at Sunset Beach, Danny?"

"Since I was twenty-four."

"Have you been singing the whole time?"

"No, that came later. At first, all I cared about was the beach scene. I just needed some cash to pay the bills. So when I moved here, I got a job as a cook at McGrady's, which is what I do during weekdays. Back when the restaurant was fairly new, maybe a year old, it didn't have much action going on inside. But I'd majored in business during college, so I found it fascinating to watch a restaurant grow from scratch. Anyway, ol' Jay hired me and paid me a tad more than minimum wage."

"Kind of hard to live off that, isn't it? No offense."

Danny shrugged. "Well, for the first few months, I survived on the money I had in savings, then got a roommate for the remainder of my lease. In the meantime, there was a retired lady who used to frequent the restaurant for lunch. I got to know her family when they visited. She decided to go live with them and offered to rent her house to me for a nominal price—and the promise that I would take care of her lawn and plants. It was a bargain, so I moved into the place when my apartment lease expired."

"So, how did your singing gig come into the picture? Did McGrady's hold auditions?"

"Actually, it was more like an accident. Jay and I became good friends, and he looked after me like an older brother. One afternoon, he stopped by my house, noticed my guitar sitting in the corner of the living room, and asked if I'd play a few licks. Apparently he liked what he heard, because he asked if I'd be interested in playing Fridays and Saturdays for extra pay. There was already a stage at McGrady's, because they'd been holding karaoke nights on the weekends."

Excited, Shannon squealed with delight. "I love karaoke!"

"Tell you what, there's nothing like watching two half-drunk guys tearing into a Bon Jovi song!" For a moment, Danny let his inhibitions go and sang a tipsy line from "Wanted Dead or Alive."

Shannon laughed, let her hands land on Danny's arms. Though the gesture itself charged his adrenaline, Danny's stomach sank. He started to recognize where her motives were headed. He'd experienced the same uninspired scenario on countless occasions at Sunset Beach.

He had to admit, she seemed so gentle and subdued as

the minutes ticked along. Yet, he couldn't ignore a disconnect between his heart and his will.

Shannon's hands lingered before falling from him in a casual, but crafted, manner. "What type of music do you perform?" she asked.

"Things that cater to a bar-and-grill environment: some Bob Dylan, a little Van Morrison, some old Peter Cetera. Plus a sampling of my own material."

"Really? How long did it take you to learn to write?"

"I was a teenager when I started—fourteen or so. Experimented with it when I was bored, and after a while, it became an addiction." Danny watched as a mother and father wrestled with their kids on the opposite side of a calm lake, three hundred feet in diameter, its shape so perfect it must have been manufactured by a contractor. The water separated The Landing into two halves, a wide footbridge their sole connection. This made the footbridge The Landing's most-traveled site. Now that closing time had passed, however, the most-traveled site sat desolate.

With tender care, Danny led Shannon by the arm. Together they stepped onto the footbridge, a composition of concrete and round pebbles. Pacing halfway across, the mismatched duo stopped to lean against the railing and catch a final glimpse of the lake, its surface rendered murky in the darkness. Danny listened to the trickle of water and the guttural croaks of frogs invisible in the night. He soaked in the image of moonlight as it sparkled upon subtle ripples of water, a sight whose beauty always left him breathless.

He wanted Meghan beside him.

Shannon's interruption came unexpected and abrupt as she shouldered him. "Look at you, concentrating so hard! Is that how you get your next song idea, by focusing like that?"

"Most often, I just sit down somewhere and start plugging away until an idea hits. But the song is most effective when I'm inspired."

"You mean by a kiss or something?"

Danny rested his chin against his locked hands. "I suppose. But more often by something less dramatic: a person walking by, an emotion, a sound I hear."

"So, anything can trigger it. Then you start playing, and you've got yourself a song?"

"Pretty much. That's simplifying it, but yeah." For a moment, Danny grew distracted by the splash of a frog as it dashed unseen through the water below. "To be honest, I've been going through some writer's block lately, where the flow plugs up like a clogged faucet. Regardless of how much time you invest, your brain stops working. And that's frustrating for a writer because they tie their purpose to it so closely." Why was he explaining this to her?

Danny peered over at Shannon, who clung to his every word. He had to admit, she looked rather beautiful as a nearby lamppost cast a sheen on her long blond hair.

"I notice a lot of singers write about a special someone," she said, breaking his train of thought.

His skin prickling, Danny grinned. "Yeah, I've done that before."

"About who?"

"A girl I knew. We were friends," he replied in a casual punt. Deciding he had revealed too much, he added. "But that was years ago."

"So you're due for another?"

"I suppose that's one way to look at it."

Tranquil and dark, The Landing was now quiet. Even the employees had departed, which left Danny and Shannon alone.

Slowly, in a silky glide that complemented the humid, intimate atmosphere, Shannon peered around and locked eyes with his. She placed her hands against his biceps, swayed his body in a gentle pivot until he faced her. Caught off guard in a moment of weakness, Danny yielded to her. He felt his back press hard against the railing. His pulse began to surge.

Danny perceived an acute hunger in Shannon's eyes, a relentless determination. Understated, yet aggressive nonetheless, it surfaced for the first time that evening. It was unmistakable.

Like a feather, Shannon slid her fingers down his arms and ribcage until her palms converged across his chest. Danny felt a rapid throb murmur within him, a nervous response to the tickle of her thumbs as she glided them over his constricting abdomen. He wondered if she could hear the pounding of his heart.

Shannon's voice grew soft and mysterious. "You know," she purred, "I think I have a way to get rid of this writer's block thing." Inching closer to him, her hand slithered beneath the waist line of his pants.

Flinching in reaction, Danny turned away and made a slow withdrawal from her touch. Though hidden in the night, he could feel his cheeks flush a feverish red. "I, uh ... I don't think so." An apprehensive chortle escaped his lips. Desperate and at a sudden loss for words, he grappled for a tension breaker. "Nothing personal, Shannon. I ... I just can't do this."

In his peripheral vision, Danny saw a shadow highlight her jaw, which grew tense. Judging from her silence, this was not the reaction she had anticipated. Such an attractive young woman couldn't be accustomed to this form of rejection, he was sure.

The awkward silence tortured him like a gouging knife.

The next minute crawled. Danny swore it was endless. Too embarrassed to make eye contact, he focused on the silhouettes of buildings on the other side of the lake. Finally, he explained, "Only one girl was able to inspire my music. Those songs were my masterpieces." Danny's mind distanced. "There hasn't been anyone since."

"Someone from around here?"

"No, from up north. I've known her my whole life."

"What's her name?"

"Meghan."

"Cute?"

"Beautiful. I think she is, anyway. Has a personality like a razor—cuts right through a person." Danny paused. "She knows me better than I know myself."

"Do you get to see her often?"

"She's with another guy. We haven't spoken in years."

Confused by this revelation, Shannon asked, "What keeps you attracted to her after all this time?"

Danny's eyes sank. "Her heart."

Silence.

Shannon stared at a random point on the water. "Sounds like an intriguing girl. Of course, *I'm* an intriguing girl too. Maybe it's time you moved on," she said. "Sounds like she has."

"Yeah," Danny muttered, then bit his lip. He was frustrated, not with the girl standing next to him, but with the girl from his past. He tried to figure when Meghan had dissolved into a sentimental apparition.

Lifting her wrist toward the moonlight, Shannon read the time. "Well, I'd better get going." After collecting a polite, mechanical hug from Danny, she took a step back. "It was nice to meet you, Danny."

"Take care, Shannon."

He looked on as she made her way to the end of the foot-bridge and disappeared into the night, into a fog that had started to creep into the summer air.

Shoving his hands into his pockets, Danny kicked the bridge railing and meandered toward the parking lot.

CHAPTER 8
JUNE 1996

Foliage crunched beneath their feet. A curled, crispy brown, the tattered leaves had battled a series of soak-and-dry cycles since settling to the ground last autumn.

From the blackness, Danny could hear the rhythmic chirps of insects that had hidden themselves among the trees. Sleeping bags in hand, he and Meghan giggled as they made their way through the shallow, backyard woods. Neither carried a flashlight. They had treaded the property throughout their childhood and knew every square inch.

Periodically looking over his shoulder, Danny watched the illumined windows of the Harting house grow tiny with distance, their fire-like glow masked by branches and tall vegetation. The scent of pollen and fungi, savory and familiar, roused his olfactory sense.

His summer euphoria halted when Meghan took an unexpected stumble, tripped by an oblong piece of tree root that had broken through the surface of the ground. Steadied by Danny's arms before she escalated to a fall, she giggled louder.

Danny released her from his grasp. "Remind me again: Which one of us lives here?"

"Shut up." She socked him in the arm as they trekked through the greenery. "I can't believe you got me out here after all this time."

Pushing aside a hanging branch, Danny exposed a small dirt area accented by scattered patches of grass. The two friends, dressed in T-shirts and grubby shorts, dropped their sleeping bags on the ground a few feet apart and began to unroll them.

"Remember when all of us used to camp out here as kids?" Meghan mused, pulling off her shoes and socks.

"You never made it through the night!"

"The company has improved since then."

After climbing into his sleeping bag, Danny reclined and locked his arms behind his head. Meghan pulled the bag to her chin, budging around inside until she found a tolerable niche. Her back would grow stiff by morning, but she was determined to endure the discomfort and remove Danny's opportunity to chide her for returning to the house before morning.

As a soft breeze rustled the trees and set the leaves flapping, a chill formed in the air. Danny and Meghan peered at the sky, caught glimpses of the moon and stars, which seemed to have aligned themselves in strategic position between tree limbs.

"The moon is so bright," Meghan said. "I wonder why it's like that some nights, but on others it's yellow or orange."

"I don't know. Probably gases or something in the atmosphere."

"I think it's beautiful."

"You know what's amazing to me?" Danny pointed at the sky. "Those things we see in the sky have been there for thousands of years. People used to ride camels and look at those stars. And that Sphinx in Egypt—maybe they worked on it during the day, then sat back and stared at that moon before falling asleep."

Captivated, Meghan crossed her arms and tried to ascertain which star was brightest. "Never occurred to me before. Weird."

"Sometimes I look up, and it hits me that there are people over in Spain or Brazil who are looking at that exact same sky at the exact same time. Wow, that's inspiring."

As Danny stared at the navy blue canvas that stretched above them, Meghan eyed him in curiosity. This was the first time she had ever heard someone speak with natural perception about such a transcendent subject. Danny seemed to possess a complex understanding of the simple.

In this unsheltered moment, Meghan swore she could hear his heartbeat. She could sense it drawing her toward him.

Without a word, Meghan glided out of her bag, her shadow elongating on the ground. In a delicate manner, she tiptoed over to Danny and lowered the zipper on his sleeping bag. Breaking his gaze from the galaxy overhead, he gazed over at his childhood friend. Her eyes communicated a tender innocence.

As Danny scooted over in silence, Meghan opened the sleeping bag and slid inside, nestled against the flannel fabric, warm from Danny's body. He removed one arm from behind his head and wrapped it around her to welcome the intrusion.

Meghan drew closer to his body and rested her hand against Danny's chest. She felt the thump of his heart against her palm, the same pattern she had sensed from across the surface of the ground.

Danny's pores bristled as Meghan eased her belly against his. Despite the onset of this uncharted physical intimacy and the fresh intrigue it had sparked between them, Danny remained calm. For the first time in her life, Meghan felt his ankle relax against her bare foot.

Minutes passed as the pair watched silver, semi-transparent clouds roll eastward in a foiled attempt to obstruct the night view.

As Danny's breath bathed hot against her face, Meghan narrowed her eyes in smugness. "I see something churning in that brain of yours."

"Just soaking everything in."

"I'll bet you could make up a song right here on the spot if you wanted to. Is that how you write?"

"I take mental pictures. Later on, when I sit down to write, I'll use one of those pictures to draw something out of my soul to amplify them. It's a process more than anything."

Meghan's jaw dropped. "Wait a minute. Are you telling me that you just write about generic stuff, when nothing urges you, and *that's* the reason my heart melts when I read those words?"

"Yep." Danny snickered.

"That's impossible."

"Why?"

"It seems so impersonal!"

"That's the way it works."

"Fine, let's hear you make something up."

"Now?"

"I want to know what's running through your 'soul' at this particular moment." When Danny hesitated, she nudged him. "Please? A song for me, just to see you in action."

Now that she had cornered him into an awkward pursuit for an idea, Danny surrendered. "All right, here's one for you: 'Behold, your beauty like the setting of the sun.'" He chuckled. "'Like a cat and mouse, you've got me on the run.'"

"That's so cheesy, I'm gonna puke!" Caught between a giggle and a gag, Meghan covered her eyes.

Danny continued his aimless stream of consciousness. "'The world is full of color today: blue, yellow, red and gray.'"

"Stop it! You win! I don't want to hear any more!"

The humor dissolved and silence resumed as the two friends laid still. As they inhaled deeper, he stroked her arm and she cuddled closer. Meghan leaned her head on his shoulder, ran her finger in tiny circles on his T-shirt. The subtle vibrations from his chest soothed her as he composed a quiet new verse:

> And as we're breathing each other's air
> Your every exhale is the hunger I bear
> I'm your man of rescue from a far, exotic land
> I'll cover you from danger with everything I can
> And I adore you

Meghan lifted her head to look at Danny, but he'd fixed his gaze on the sky above. Though physically still, he seemed somehow in motion, mysterious.

> When the air warms your skin
> When the tides are rushing in
> When the stars are in the sky
> Shining down for you and I

As he created exclusive poetry for her, Meghan examined him in close detail: The contours of his face, aglow with cascades of moonlight. The clear passion in his eyes. The way his lips parted as words dripped from his mouth, fluid like wine.

> When the waters understand
> When they're moving through your hands

Washing over you
When the moon serenades you

Rapt in thought, Danny grew silent.

Meghan's lower lip quivered. Danny was one of the few people she allowed to see her weak with emotional vulnerability.

"Well," she whispered, "you did it again."

Severing his personal trance, Danny turned his head and focused into her face. "Hmm?"

Meghan wiped a tear that had started to form. Sniffling, she looked straight into his eyes. "You just broke my heart."

Danny paused for a moment, then nodded. The trace of a smile fluttered at the corner of his mouth. He wrapped his other arm around her and held her close. Pressing into his chest, she felt his gentle kiss on her head.

Meghan closed her eyes.

She felt safe.

CHAPTER 9
JUNE 2007

With books strewn in assorted piles across the living room floor, Brian sorted through the contents of one bookcase while the other begged for his attention. He and Meghan had stuffed both beyond capacity with novels and textbooks collected over the years. Each shelf contained one neat row of books with several sloppy stacks hidden behind it. Between sneezes, Brian flipped through each dusty book, depositing the less desirable ones in a cardboard box for their new destination in the basement.

Purse in hand, Meghan entered the room in a whirlwind, darting past him as she selected her car key. "I'm running to the store. Back later." Glancing over her shoulder, she added, "Don't clean those by yourself. I'll pitch in later."

In an effort to catch her, Brian rushed to grab a hardcover novel, which he'd isolated from the others.

"Babe!" he shouted.

Already in the garage, Meghan poked her head back through the door.

Brian waved the novel in the air. "What's this?"

Shutting the door, Meghan walked over and took a look

at the hardcover he handed her. Though she recognized the title, the plot eluded her. She shuffled through the pages, then removed a letter that stuck out from between the pages.

Meghan shook the flimsy envelope, which couldn't have contained more than a single page. Postmarked in Charlotte, North Carolina, in late 1997, it was addressed to Meghan at the apartment where she had lived at the time. The return address contained no name, but she recognized the street as Danny Bale's college address.

"Where did you find this?" she asked.

"It was stuck in the middle of the book."

"Did you read the letter?"

"No. Why? Is that the guy you used to keep in touch with?"

Meghan furled her eyebrows. "Looks like it. I forgot I even had this."

A glare of sarcasm in his eyes, Brian asked, "Are you sure?"

She waved the envelope at him. "Look at the postmark, Brian. It's from ten years ago."

"You must've wanted it around for some reason."

"I think you're making a big deal out of it. I told you, I don't remember it."

"You had it shoved in the back of the shelf."

Meghan rolled her eyes. "Along with all the other books that old."

"The others didn't have letters hidden inside."

"Brian, you and I didn't even start dating until almost a year later. I probably used it as a bookmark."

"So you never finished this novel?"

"That depends. How did it end?"

"Very funny."

"Look," Meghan said, ripping the envelope into shreds.

"Does this make you happy?"

Brian responded with a shrug. "Whatever floats your boat, babe."

In a refusal to pursue the argument further, Meghan thrust the novel back at him. "I'm leaving. Do you need anything while I'm out?"

"No." Brian tossed the book into the box with a handful of others. The letter, now confetti, remained scattered around him.

Meghan stared at him but received no further acknowledgement. No doubt this discovery would serve as a topic of future conversation, followed by a remark on how she refused to divulge additional details.

She closed the door behind her.

• • •

The bedroom was dark. Meghan flipped on a small table lamp. Out entertaining a client until late, Brian wouldn't return for hours.

Meghan walked over to her closet and slid the door open. She knelt down and began to dig through shoeboxes stacked along the closet's inner wall. Delving deeper, she retrieved a yellow shoebox. Much heavier than the others, its lid struggled to remain in place atop its body, which bulged at the sides.

Sitting cross-legged on the thick carpet, she lifted the lid to uncover a collection of letters and cards, now several years old. Already the ink on the envelopes had started to fade with the passage of time. Each item was postmarked in either Charlotte, North Carolina, or Solon, Ohio, and each had arrived from Danny Bale.

Meghan pulled from the box a random card, which she recognized as a birthday card. She chuckled as she ran her finger over the inferior drawing that Danny had added to one page. Next, near the front of the shoebox, she found a letter Danny had sent during his first week at college.

When had she last perused these old letters? She couldn't recall. One by one, in no particular order, she removed letters from the box, read them, and relished the memories she associated with each. To her surprise, she could even recall where she had sat when she had first read many of them. Some sparkled with clarity from being printed on a printer, while others, handwritten and torn from a spiral notebook, contained ragged edges. Many of the envelopes were thick with pages of lyrics Danny had written during his college years.

But as Brian came to Meghan's mind, she felt a sense of guilt overshadow her enjoyment of memories involving Danny. In a hurry, as if Brian's car could arrive home at any moment, Meghan removed bunches of letters at once, spreading the envelope edges apart to give herself a quick, final glance at the contents. Bypassing all cards, she searched for a specific envelope.

She found it. An oversized envelope, folded in thirds.

Hoping to catch a lingering whiff of Danny's cologne, she lifted the envelope to her nose, but time and storage had rendered the scent dead. As expected, when she removed its contents, she found a song attached to Danny's letter. However, unlike the songs he'd attached to other letters, Danny had prepared sheet music for this one, which Meghan examined anew. Her eyes settled at the top of the composition. Meghan smiled as she read the title, one she had never forgotten.

"Meghan's Song."

Meghan placed the other letters back in the box and returned it to the back of the closet, where she used other shoeboxes to camouflage it. She made her way to the dresser, where she dropped the envelope into her purse and zipped it shut.

Her jaw firm, Meghan left the bedroom, turning off the light behind her.

CHAPTER 10
JUNE 2007

On this Saturday, in the early afternoon, Danny found the bus station's population sparse, just as he'd expected. Once a staple in the area, the small building now risked falling victim to a bulldozer due to commercialization efforts. According to rumor, a national hotel chain salivated at a possible land purchase.

Next to the station, Danny sat in an all-purpose shop that combined a convenience store and self-serve diner—a truck stop without the trucks. The bus station and shop shared a common roof. A rectangular hole in the wall, a remnant of a door removed years before, connected the two businesses. Occupying a booth at one of two tables, Danny sipped a cup of stale coffee. Gritty and lukewarm, the beverage had cost him three dollars thanks to the *Premium Java!* sign that hung above the dusty urn.

He didn't care about the coffee, though. He was on the look-out for the next bus.

Through a filthy window, Danny watched as residents from nearby towns awaited the same overdue bus arrival. Their facial expressions split between eagerness and impatience as they checked their watches every two minutes. Danny fiddled with a pair of salt and pepper shakers and wondered how many greasy hands had touched the same cloudy, glass pieces. With the table in obvious neglect since the shop opened for the day, he grabbed a napkin from the metal dispenser and brushed away salt crystals in an effort to pass the time.

Downing the last sip, Danny refused to ingest the grainy silt that remained. He tossed the cardboard cup into the trash and browsed the various quotes on a rack of foam-and-web trucker hats. Fitted with the qualities of a rustic town, the outskirts of Sunset Beach had inspired a couple of songs for Danny, despite the humor he derived from this section of the neighborhood. Who would expect to find mini-golf and roller coasters a few miles away?

Opening the shop's front door, Danny triggered the make-shift burglar alarm—a string of jingle bells that hung from the door handle. The cashier didn't look up. Danny meandered into the humidity outside, where instant beads of perspiration burst across his forehead and trickled to his cheeks. He put on his sunglasses and waited.

When the silver bus approached, an elderly couple with matching white hair emerged from the shade of a nearby bench and waved with excitement. The bus squealed to a stop, its doors opened, and a handful of passengers stepped down. Close behind a group of retirees, a man in military garb carried a duffel bag and surveyed the locals.

Danny grinned and hurried toward the bus.

Eyeing him, the military officer sported a mischievous grin. When they met halfway, he greeted Danny with a solid hug and a firm pat on the back. "How's it going, little brother?"

"Good to see ya, Reece."

After living away from his family for a decade, a portion of it on foreign soil, Reece often noted how his appreciation for family had multiplied. After a recent relocation to an army base in Kentucky, he now spent his days training recruits. A dirty tan revealed that this man with the cropped hair invested a great deal of time in outdoor instruction.

Danny seized the duffel bag from his brother's hand and motioned toward the car. "Come on, let's go."

• • •

Just after one in the morning, Reece grabbed a bag of potato chips from Danny's pantry and headed into the living room. Dressed in a comfortable orange T-shirt and shorts, he padded barefoot to the sofa and plopped down on his back. Danny, slouched in the armchair, flipped through television channels to catch sports highlights. Two years had passed since the brothers had seen each other.

The room was dark, save the glow from the television and a dim lamp beside the armchair. Danny had left the window open for the night. A draft teased the blinds and caused them to rattle.

"This is what I call a weekend getaway," Reece said. "The sun, the beach—you know how to live in style, man."

"I don't ever want to see that Ohio snow again." Danny shivered in disgust at the thought.

"Where did those years go?" Reece sat up, his eyes alive. "Remember that time back in Solon when Meghan had us changing seats in the moving vehicle?"

"Aw, dude, you're lucky you're still alive. Seriously."

"Yeah, life didn't seem so risky after that. She put me in

danger long before the military ever put a weapon in my hands!" They laughed together.

Pondering for a moment, Danny asked, "Whatever happened to her?"

"Meghan? Last I heard, she moved in with that Brian guy. She works at an apartment complex, I think." Reece popped a potato chip into his mouth. "Funny how you lose touch with people over time. I never think to ask Mom or Dad. When did you last talk to her?"

"I sent a letter when I first moved to the beach. Never heard back from her." Danny scratched his late-night stubble. He never asked his parents or brothers about Meghan. He believed he'd look ridiculous, still thinking about her in a romantic way after all this time. "Think she's married by now?"

"No, she's definitely single. Sent me a Christmas card—just a card, no details on her life. But she signed it with her maiden name."

Surprised at the news, wheels turned inside Danny's head. How could it be possible? Meghan and Brian had started their relationship during Danny's latter days in college. Surely there was more to the story.

The flickering TV light must have cast a blue tint of betrayal upon Danny's face, because Reece fixed his gaze on his brother, who stared at a random point in space.

"When was the last time you went home, Dan?"

"To Ohio?" Danny started to count holidays. "Easter or something. You were there too, so a couple of years, I guess."

"Not even Christmas or Thanksgiving?"

"I hate the cold."

"So you stay away?" Reece snapped his fingers. "Just like that?"

"What's the difference? You haven't gone there either, have you?"

"That's not the same. I just got back to the states. I plan to get home this year. Besides, aren't you the least bit curious about what's changed?"

"It makes me numb to go back there. When I left, it was permanent for me."

"Well, it's not like your old job is waiting to suck you back into your former lifestyle."

Danny contemplated against further explanation but surrendered in the end. "That wasn't the only thing I left behind. Granted, I hated that career. But truth be told, I was looking for an excuse to leave town, and that mortgage job provided a reason that seemed halfway justifiable."

A barrage of pressure settled around Danny's brain. In a manic daze, he found himself trying to weave together the strands of his life—the past, the present, and everything in between—until, at last, his heart dropped.

"I loved her, Reece. When I lost the prospect of Meghan, I lost something in my fiber." Danny pounded his chest with a fist. "Something that makes me who I am." Suddenly, Danny felt exposed. Embarrassed, he shook his head and said, "Geez, that sounds so stupid. I can't believe I just said that."

Reece didn't utter a word. Although Danny wanted to keep quiet, he grew overwhelmed with frustration. After years in suppression, it now bubbled hot within him.

"I'm the one who stood by her," Danny said. "The baby, the abandonment of the kid's father—all of it. I saw who she was, past the harsh façade, and I *loved* her for what I saw." Palms open, Danny shook his head in disbelief. "How could she not recognize that? It blows me away."

"Everyone gets their heart broken at some point, Dan. Nothing out of the ordinary there."

"I know." Danny fell back in the armchair. "I thought I had gotten over her, that's all."

Danny's mind traveled through years past, making split-second pit stops at random points along the way. For some reason, minor details now started to increase in stature and amass greater relevance.

"You know what the irony of this whole situation is?" Danny asked. "Most people would walk outside my back door, watch the ocean waves roll, soak in the sun, and call it paradise." Danny stared at a dark window across the room. "I used to see it that way too. I thought I could escape the ache by coming down here, figured I'd physically remove myself from anywhere near Meghan's vicinity." Danny shot his brother a clever smirk, one that insinuated wisdom gained through hindsight. "It worked for the first couple of years," he said, his eyes narrowing as if to mimic an unsuspecting fool.

"So what changed?"

"This whole paradise thing started to get lonely because it's meant to be shared."

"A lot of people wouldn't even have made the move like you did."

"It didn't get me very far. Take a look, Reece: I'm a college-educated *cook!* I have my music and not much else." Danny thumped the edge of the chair with his finger. "I never pictured myself stuck at this age. I thought I'd want to move on after a couple of years. The weird thing is, something prevents me from reaching forward. It's like an invisible brick wall right in front of my face, blocking my future. And that wall is ten feet thick."

Setting the bag of chips on the coffee table, Reece leaned forward on the sofa. "I'm gonna tell you something: When I was serving overseas, it was an honor. There was a higher purpose to it—but it was still dangerous. Believe me, the whole time I was there, I was glad I had a weapon on me. And if a threat became serious, I used that weapon." He locked eyes with Danny. "Music is your weapon, Dan. When you're in a crunch, you've got that gun in your arsenal." Gesturing at Danny, he said, "I mean, the way you look at things—it's different from other people. You sense things that other people are clueless about. You have this uncanny ability to put words to things that no one else is able to say."

"I sing every weekend, Reece. It's a blast, but it doesn't provide a solution for the future."

"You don't understand. Listen to me: Songwriting is your outlet. When you're trapped in a hole, that's the shovel you use to dig yourself out." Sinking back against the cushion, he added, "And if I were you, I'd start digging. With all the strength I've got, I'd force myself out."

"I suppose. Find a way to press forward with the future and let the past fall in place, huh?"

Reece grinned. "Well … before you can move ahead with your future, maybe there's a part of you that needs to settle things from the past."

Though an inkling of resolve stirred inside, Danny felt helpless. "Every part of me believed Meghan and I were destined for each other. Permanently linked. Created that way."

"Weren't there times you doubted it?"

"Never. I was so confident about it, like there was iron in my backbone." Raising his eyebrows, he said, "I was going to marry her."

"Wait, what do you mean?"

"I was planning my life with her back in college. When I took those finance classes, I was planning investment strategies to send our kids through school. I sat in class and listened to the lectures, weighed different mortgage options for our first house. And on Saturdays, when I would sit in a fast-food restaurant and study, it became so real to me: I was getting a degree so I could support a wife I loved and the kids that would arrive down the road."

"Do you ever wish you'd stuck around Ohio and earned an annual salary so you could reach those financial goals? The slightest desire?"

"It didn't matter anymore. My dreams were already shot. When the prospect of Meghan disappeared, I lost *everything*, because I lost a part of who I am." Chuckling, he said, "After all these years, how can a person be in love with someone he never took out on a single date?"

"That's not a shocker, Dan. You two were close friends, and you knew her better than anyone else." Reece paused, a glint in his eye. "Even Brian."

That comment aroused Danny's curiosity. He had never considered such a notion, but he knew it to be true. Which led to Danny's next question: Could it be possible that nothing had changed in that respect?

Danny turned toward his brother, who had already shifted his attention.

Reece grabbed the bag of potato chips again, searching for an extra crunchy victim.

CHAPTER 11
JANUARY 1997

Danny tried to carry an oversized box from the corner of Meghan's den. Within seconds, his lopsided trek deteriorated to an uncontrollable hop. As he leaned his leg against Meghan's couch to catch his balance, the box slipped out of his grasp and landed on the floor with a thud. Cutting his losses, he decided to drag it to the center of the room instead.

"Good thing those weren't breakable," Meghan chided.

Danny opened the box and sifted inside. "Unbelievable," he said. "You packed about a hundred pounds' worth of weights into this!"

"Yeah, I'm into aerobics now."

"I guess so."

"Do you want me to get a *man* to move it?"

"Shut up."

After moving Meghan into her new apartment, Danny had turned down her father's lunch offer, opting to spend the extra time with Meghan instead. Danny ignored his grumbling stomach and unloaded the dumbbells, rolling them beneath the couch where, knowing Meghan, she would rediscover them a year later.

"You've gotta see what I picked up yesterday," Meghan said. She lifted a two-piece infant outfit from a shopping bag. "Isn't this adorable?"

Danny tried to picture the miniature body that would fit into the canary-yellow costume, the front of which featured an etching of a rubber duck. He watched Meghan tug at the tiny sleeves and couldn't recall when he'd last seen her so exuberant. A mere seven weeks into her pregnancy, she had already launched into mother mode and seldom talked about anything else.

Returning the clothes to the bag, Meghan marched with it to her freshly painted bedroom, another addition to the nest. On her way back, she grabbed two cans of cola from the refrigerator and handed one to Danny. "Here, take a break."

Danny popped it open and sat beside her on the couch. "Congratulations," he said, then took his first sip. The carbonation tickled his throat and invigorated him. "Now you have an excuse for another spending spree."

"Within reason. I'm on a budget—one more mouth to feed soon."

"Are you worried at all?"

Meghan shrugged. "Nah. I was, but not anymore."

"Everything's falling into place?"

"Yeah. Plus, the situation has smoothed over with my parents. That was the biggest hurdle."

"How'd they take it when you broke the news to them?"

"Totally speechless at first. My dad could've caught flies in his mouth, wide open as it was. They both tried to hide any reaction, acting like it was totally normal." Meghan flicked the side of her can. Her eyes grew distant. "I could see the disappointment in their eyes—especially Dad's. His little girl finally screwed up big time, but I'm sure he expected it to happen eventually."

"But they seem comfortable with the idea now?"

Meghan's eyes returned to life. "Are you kidding? Mom is thrilled. She's been out every day getting ideas for toys and supplies. She always wanted to be a grandma; it just came a tad early. I have total support from both of them, though, which is more than I can say for my so-called friends."

"Why? Are they giving you grief about the pregnancy?"

"They took off," Meghan replied, tongue wedged against her cheek. "All of them. Won't even talk to me, like I'm a leper."

"Very nice." Danny wished he lived closer.

"You know what makes me angry, though? I hung out with those people all through high school and listened to their sob stories. And where are they now?" From the way her jaw locked, Danny could tell she fumed inside. Meghan took another swallow. "Small as Oxford is, it's hard not to run into a few of them here and there. They're so pathetic. Wouldn't dare make eye contact with the girl who got herself pregnant. They never have anything to say—not to my face, anyway. All I hear is *'psst, psst'* from the other side of the room." Meghan waved her hands in front of her in clear sarcasm. "Ooh, I'll never figure out what *that* conversation's all about!"

Danny peered into her blue eyes, then saw directly through them. Though her veneer seemed polished like shiny, stalwart armor, Danny recognized one truth Meghan would leave unspoken: Her former friends had wounded her to the core, and the scars they had left were permanent, or at least long-term.

"I'll think twice before trusting people again," Meghan said. "Except you."

Today, Danny witnessed a fresh dimension to his friend and

noted its significance. They had grown up in regular contact with each other, but he couldn't recall a time when she had exposed her soul so openly. Her resilient personality was more than a trait; it had become her defense mechanism over time, preventing outsiders from penetrating her skin and bruising her heart. Yet now, perhaps by accident, she had chosen to allow Danny in. He felt like an invited guest.

As he listened to her words, Danny perceived within himself a void. A smooth hole he had never noticed before. A subtle groove for which, somehow, Meghan provided the perfect fit.

And here, in the simplicity of the moment, he felt his heart bond with hers. With the delicacy of an artist's touch, a revelation seeped into his soul.

Danny loved Meghan deeply.

For Danny, the realization came without emotion. Instead, it tugged at his senses, yearned for his attention. As if to overshadow the innocent attraction he'd felt toward her in the past, the roots of his newfound love for her had disseminated to his every fiber. A mysterious draw enabled him to view her with unconditional eyes. Meghan was about to birth another man's child, and Danny couldn't care less. His heart was connected to hers.

Danny jostled her knee. "How is your ex-boyfriend handling the idea of being a father?"

Meghan shook her head. "Eric? He's gone too." No emotion, just matter of fact.

"You gave him the news and he abandoned you?"

"Well, to his credit, it didn't happen that fast," Meghan said. "I didn't want to worry Eric for nothing, so when I suspected something, I took a home pregnancy test. It turned out positive. The next time he and I saw each other, I broke the news to him."

"How'd he react?"

"He broke out in a sweat, then said, 'Let's try another test to make sure.' Next thing you know, we're walking into the drugstore and he buys me another test—different brand. He paid for it himself."

"Big spender."

"Anyway," Meghan poked his arm, "that test turned out negative. Eric was relieved and ready to move on like normal. But you always hear about people getting different results, so I made an appointment with the OB-GYN without telling Eric. I showed up at the doctor's office, went through the routine, and it turned out the pregnancy was real. As relieved as Eric had acted when the home test had turned out negative, it was obvious he didn't want fresh news of a pregnancy. I didn't know what to do, but I also knew I couldn't keep it a secret. The rumors would start to circulate."

"Among your *psst-psst* friends," Danny joshed.

"Yeah." Meghan rolled her eyes. "Well, I drove straight to Eric's house and told him."

"Was he angry that you made the appointment behind his back?"

"No, but he was in total denial mode. And that's understandable because, at that point, he was probably in shock. As I'd expected, he'd counted on a false alarm. He tried every question he could think of to dance around the facts." Grabbing Danny's arm, Meghan's eyes widened. "He even asked if the baby was his!"

Danny grunted with disgust.

Meghan seemed to handle the notion in a straightforward manner. "I told him, 'Of course it's yours!' I mean, I know I've done some stupid things, but I don't sleep around." Meghan fingered the tab on her cola can, kept her eyes glued to it. "I told him I didn't expect anything from him. I didn't want any money, and I didn't want to force a baby on him." She paused, then added, "He put my hand in his and told me, 'I'm gonna stand by you, Meghan. Whatever you need, I'm there.' Well, I felt like he'd taken a load off my shoulders. I was so confused because everything had happened fast. I mean, all of a sudden, our lives had turned upside down, and we had a ton of decisions to make. One night you're going to a movie, the next night you find out you're pregnant. What a relief not to wade through it alone!"

Meghan crossed her arms and appeared to shiver. Danny just listened as she spoke. Uninvolved in the daily step-by-step of her life, he'd never grown acquainted with how Meghan responded to challenges. Today his respect for her mounted higher.

Meghan opened her mouth to speak further, but hesitated. Curling her legs on the couch, Meghan gave her toenail polish a nervous examination before she spoke again. "Eric must have gotten scared when the idea of fatherhood sunk in, because when I called the next day, he told me he'd been doing some thinking. He wants to be an accountant for a Fortune 500 company, and a baby doesn't fit into his life right now." When she peered up at Danny, she bit her lower lip and tried to fend off a film of tears that glistened upon her eyes. "That's when Eric said, 'Don't call me anymore.'"

Danny winced. Immediately his heart felt sore. "Those were his words?"

Meghan clenched her jaw, enunciated each syllable: "Verbatim."

Danny sighed, a reaction laced with incomprehension. How could he respond to what Meghan had just told him? How could Eric have treated her in such a way, as if to wipe the ink from his hands after touching a ragged newspaper?

"What a jerk," Danny said. Anger raced like venom through Danny's veins. Yet, even though he seethed inside, he determined to remain calm. He didn't want to upset Meghan or the child inside her.

Meghan relaxed her shoulders. "The baby's better off without him. If that's how little he cared, he would've walked away at *some* point, so it's better he did it right away. The baby doesn't deserve to get hurt like that later on."

"So Eric let you face your parents alone, I take it?"

"Yeah, but like I said before, it turned out okay. It was hard, but sometimes you just need to press through things. Besides, if I couldn't tell my own parents, how would I manage to give birth?"

"So it's you, your family, and me, huh?"

Meghan raised her eyebrows. "Actually, I've gotten to know someone else recently. His name is Brian. He works in Cincinnati, an advertising prodigy. We've dated once or twice but have become friends. I can't imagine moving beyond that. He's been nothing but supportive." Meghan nudged Danny and grinned. "Brian listens to a lot of this rambling I've subjected *you* to!"

"Well, it's good you have someone close by, I suppose." To Danny, his own physical distance from Meghan seemed less than fair.

She nodded, her face beaming. "Anyway," she said, "this is so exciting! Nowadays, whenever I make a decision, I ask myself, 'Would this be the right choice if the baby were here?'"

"You'll be a terrific mom."

Meghan rested her elbows on her knees, her chin upon her clasped hands. "I look forward to the little things the most: my child's first step, serving up those teeny jars of baby food, then the soccer games, the swimming lessons—"

"Hey, you can be a PTA mom!"

Bullet-fast, Meghan sat up straight. "Absolutely! How fun would *that* be? And now and then, we'll even drive up north to visit Uncle Danny!"

Danny watched Meghan's eyes gleam as her creativity sparked. She was beautiful.

Meghan's expression straightened again. "Wait a minute! You'll be away at college by that time. Have you decided where?"

"I got an early acceptance to the University of North Carolina in Charlotte."

"Well, you'll have to give me your address when you get it. We definitely need to keep in touch. And I'll keep you updated with pictures of the baby."

"Do you have email?"

"A computer's not in the budget, buddy boy."

"Oh."

"Besides, I want to scrutinize your handwriting and try to find the subliminal messages. Artistic interpretation, like when you look at a painting. I'll figure out what you're *really* thinking behind those words of yours."

As Meghan allowed her imagination to dance, Danny glanced down at her belly and marveled at the notion that a child hid somewhere beneath the layers. As he pictured the pain Meghan would endure during childbirth and the sacrifices she would make to care for her baby, Danny's affection for Meghan continued to rise.

Then it dawned on him: In a matter of months, her toned

belly would carry evidence that a pregnancy had occurred. While this would cause many men to keep their distance from her, Danny found it attractive. In his own mind, her stressed belly would symbolize the life to which she had given birth and the love with which she had covered her child before he—or she—took its first breath.

CHAPTER 12
JUNE 2007

"Order in!" shouted a waitress as she clipped a ticket to the line of incoming orders.

Situated between the noise of a diminishing crowd and the clanging of cooking utensils, Danny grabbed the next ticket and started to build a spicy dish of shrimp and pasta. Beside him, Jay performed grill duty, working magic on a chicken breast and a pair of burger patties. With the time approaching two in the afternoon, Jay had released Danny's other cohorts for the day.

As garlic cloves sautéed in butter, the aroma triggered hunger pangs in Danny's stomach. Hours ago, he had planned his late-lunch selection for when he caught up with orders from straggling customers. The scent at hand, however, stimulated new ideas.

Jay placed a patty on a toasted bun, then accented it with a mound of shredded lettuce. Jay shuddered at the uninspiring configuration.

"I tell ya, Danny Boy, some people just don't live on the edge. Check this out."

More concerned with his own growling stomach, Danny glanced at the burger anyway. Jay flicked his hand at the sight before him as he held up the order ticket. He rapped his finger at each ingredient detail. "One McGrady's cheeseburger. No onion, no pickle, no mayo, no mustard, no adventure at the beach." He slapped the ticket down on the stainless-steel counter. The resulting sound reminded Danny of a gong that might announce an emperor's arrival. "Should I ask 'em if they'd like a bun with that?"

Clearly amused with his own comment, Jay shook his head. He finished the other burger and shoved both plates onto the ledge, where a prompt waitress carried it off to the uncreative soul who awaited it.

Jay reached for the next ticket and tossed another burger on the grill. The initial sizzling began. "So what was the deal with Shannon the other night? You didn't like her?"

Danny added shrimp and chives to the melted butter and tossed them around. "She wasn't my type, I guess."

"You mean my instincts were wrong?"

"With all due respect, you saw her getting a manicure and built your case from there."

"I hear the carousel operator is looking for someone."

Danny laughed. "Tell you what, I appreciate it, but I'll let you have the carousel operator all to yourself."

"You have to admit, that Shannon's got it going on."

Danny shrugged off Jay's observation. "A great body is fine," Danny replied, focusing on the shrimp in front of him. "But one day, she'll turn eighty years old, and it'll go downhill from there. Gravity, you know."

"I hear ya."

"At this point, I'm looking for substance in a woman. More than blond in a bottle."

"You always were the smartest one working at this place."

Danny emptied the garlic shrimp into a bowl of pasta, mixed the ingredients together, and scraped them onto a dish. As he garnished the entrée, he debated whether to extend the current conversation, then decided to plunge forward. "Jay, what do you think about destiny?"

"You mean Destiny Landing?"

"No, like *fate*. Things happening for a reason. Finding your soul mate, that one person you're going to spend your life with."

"You're not going to grab my hand, are ya, Dan?"

"Seriously."

Jay stopped grilling for a moment. He regarded Danny for a moment, scrunched his lip, then flipped the burger.

In a forthright tone, Jay replied, "All right, if you really wanna know, here's the way I see it." Jay pointed to the patty with his spatula and said, "Take a look at this hamburger. A lot of things could happen to it. This burger could be destined for bacon, lettuce, and tomato. Or maybe it's destined for grilled onions and cheddar." He widened his hands, spread his fingers in mock excitement. "Or it could be destined for jalapeno peppers. Get my drift?"

A bewildered stare. "No, man. I don't."

Jay pounded his fist into his other hand. "What I'm trying to say is this: Destiny is whatever you make of it. I think it's all in your own hands." Removing the burger from the grill, he shoveled it onto a plate to add its garnishing. "And some people have the balls to go for the jalapenos."

Intrigued, Danny folded his arms, astounded at the sudden dose of insight that had oozed from shaggy Jay McGrady's mouth. "So, you don't believe that your life is simply meant for a specific course?"

Jay turned toward him. His face, though laced with an

expression of humor, also gleamed with sweat, flushed crimson from the fiery grill. "Danny, take a look at me. I'm thirty-five years old, flipping burgers at my parents' restaurant. Don't you think I would've gotten another job by now if I really wanted to?" He reached out his arms to span the abstract horizon before him. Jay's eyes carried an air of sinister cleverness. "All the other shops at this landing peddle their saltwater taffy and souvenir key chains, and they can't fathom why on earth an unsightly, bare-wooded, music-blaring bar with a bunch of tables is the most popular joint here. And I'm gonna inherit this place from my family's blood, sweat and tears. And it's because I *chose* to make it my destiny. Some people think I'm nuts, but hey, lick me, because this is my destiny and I wouldn't trade it for anything."

Wiping his hands on a towel, Danny mulled over his friend's remarks and started to piece together the events that had brought him to Sunset Beach, fitting them into the scenario in which he lived today. His fascination with song had been the peak of his joy during his tenure at the shore. The sun's balmy glow had kept him alert, eager to pursue his craft.

In the end, however, Danny was alone.

Jay stared ahead at the flames, which jumped from the grill and teased another chicken breast. With one eye on Jay, Danny said nothing, noting that Jay had shifted into a mode of discreet concentration.

"Look, Dan, you're my most valuable employee, so don't take this the wrong way," Jay said at last. "You're welcome to work here as long as you want. You've got a strong work ethic, and you're a killer act on stage."

With the back of his forearm, Danny wiped the perspiration from his own brow. At an apparent loss for words, Jay was in rare form. The same Jay McGrady that had guided Danny upon his arrival at the beach now seemed to lurk behind minimal eye contact.

Jay continued, "You could be doing so much more, guy. I mean, you have a college degree. Instead of singing at a bar, why not own a record company?" Jay poked at the chicken. "You're kidding yourself if you think you can spend the rest of your life living here. All along, I knew the day would come when I'd see you leave. And I want you to know that whatever step you want to take, you have my full support." Jay halted. He chuckled as he looked Danny straight in the eyes. "What are you doing here, Dan? This place isn't real. It's a bunch of sand and photographs. Great for visitors and business owners, but beyond that, it's not going anywhere. And you deserve more than that. Just some big-brother advice."

"I'm doing fine."

"No, you're not—you don't have the same *mmph* you had before, and that probably means you're supposed to do something that you haven't started yet. Talk about destiny, man! Whatever that is, move forward with it. If you're holding on to something, you may need to let go, then let 'er rip." Jay scraped some crust from the grill, then added, "And no, you can't have a raise."

CHAPTER 13
JUNE 2007

Meghan wasn't too familiar with Miami University's Center for Performing Arts building, having only entered it twice. She had taken a course in music appreciation, but the large class had met in another building, in an auditorium surrounded by the stench of biological science.

The scent inside this Center was much tamer. Now that the semester had ended, the hallways were silent. As she walked along, she noticed that, while the Center carried a cultured flavor, it still possessed an institutional feel reminiscent of a fancy, albeit empty, high school. The ambience struck her as unnatural.

Upon checking the name plate at the door, Meghan tapped on the cold, metal threshold of a compact office, where a curly-haired woman in her early forties clicked away on a computer keyboard. Breaking concentration, the woman removed her wire-rimmed glasses and smiled.

"How's it going, Christine?"

An associate professor in the Department of Music, Christine Kelker possessed an extraordinary aptitude for learning a musical instrument in minimal time, from the cello to the harmonica. Meghan's father had introduced her to Christine after meeting the musical connoisseur at a university reception several years ago. Though they were not close friends, Meghan and Christine had become regular acquaintances while passing each other on the campus sidewalks.

Christine tucked a lock of hair, its auburn tone highlighted by isolated strands of gray, behind her ear. "What a coincidence you're here! I just asked your dad how you're doing. Bumped into him yesterday."

"Everything's fine." Meghan glanced at the wall, where a clock read 5:52 p.m. "It's going on dinner time. I didn't know if I'd catch you before you left for the day."

"Have a seat." Christine waved at a chair on the other side of her desk. "With things so bogged down right now, I'm liable to be here till nine tonight. But this is a nice distraction! What brings you by?"

Meghan sat down on a wooden chair accented with insti-tutional-green fabric. Reaching into her purse, she removed Danny's large envelope. "I was wondering if you'd mind playing some music for me."

"Sure thing. I could use a break from these semester grades anyway. What do you have?"

"It's a song a friend sent to me."

"A guy?"

"Yeah, long time ago. I don't play an instrument; otherwise, I'd do this myself."

Christine nibbled on the tip of her eyeglasses. "Did he know you couldn't play?"

"Yeah, but he told me he needed to send the full song in order to do it justice."

Christine's eyes bloomed. "Have you ever heard anyone play it?"

"Never."

"Let's take a look." Holding out her hand, Christine put her glasses on again.

Meghan pulled the sheet music from the envelope and handed it across the desk, where Christine grasped it and settled back in her squeaky, faux-leather chair.

When she read the title, Christine raised her eyebrows and glanced over at Meghan. "'Meghan's Song.' Hmm ..." she teased, growing wispy at the topic. "A song written exclusively for Meghan. Have you ever shown this to anyone?"

Meghan shook her head. Not only had she never shown the song to anyone, no one else knew it existed. A personal treasure, Meghan had regarded it as private.

Eyes darting back and forth, top to bottom, Christine turned the pages, scanning each one and comparing segments with those of prior pages. After perusing the final page, Christine nodded, then clucked her tongue in a studious manner. "Very interesting." Rising from her chair, she said, "There should be an open practice room. Let's see what this sounds like on a keyboard."

Meghan followed Christine out the door and down the hall. Arriving at a collection of tiny rooms, Christine turned on a light in the nearest one, exposing a lone piano-style keyboard that entertained an audience of two fabric-lined chairs. The lighting was bright, but the room was cold, which left Meghan with a sense of claustrophobia. She crossed her arms as goose bumps poked along the surface of her flesh.

Christine shut the door, took her seat at the keyboard stool, and spread the pages of music before her. Meghan stepped backward toward the corner of the room and stood at an angle behind Christine. Unable to predict her own reaction upon hearing the song, she wanted to avoid letting Christine see the outcome. At the moment, Meghan would have given anything to play the song herself in a private setting. Yet, she couldn't bear to wait any longer. Revisiting the song had also unleashed a relentless need to reconnect with this facet of her past, a sojourn long overdue.

Staring at Danny's penciled notes, Christine tackled the chords and melody first. Line by line, she plunked through the composition, repeating botched combinations, doubling and tripling her attempts at critical points, humming along with the melody. At face value, her method appeared unimpressive.

Meghan watched.

When patterns began to emerge, Christine announced, "I have a feel for where he's headed with this. It's a basic arrangement—chords, melody, bass line. What instrument does he play?"

"Guitar."

"With both hands mobile on a keyboard, I can maneuver around the tune better. I'm going to flower it up a bit to enhance the flavor of what he's communicating to you."

Meghan nodded her approval. A key reason for Christine's musical proficiency, Meghan knew, was her ability to play music by ear. Once before, Meghan had seen someone play music on first sight and had marveled at such talent.

Turning the pages to the beginning once again, Christine swayed to the rhythm as she played. Though the song resembled the original form Meghan had just heard, the tones now seemed to approach from different angles and converge at the ivory keys.

This time, however, Meghan trembled as she allowed the tune to sweep over her. As the lyrics poured forth from

Christine's mouth, Meghan's heart palpitated, rapid and uncontrolled, beneath her skin. A lump in her throat made swallowing difficult. Meghan fought her tears but wound up unsuccessful as they trickled down her cheeks. Some slid down her neck, others settled on her lips like a salty balm. Danny's words crept into Meghan's ears and pierced her heart.

Without his presence in the room, she could sense him touching her.

For the first time in her life, Meghan now heard a song written from his soul to hers. Danny expressed himself best through music, yet she had never listened to this song written solely for her. Although she had read its lyrics more times than she could count, she now understood why Danny had needed to send her the complete composition. The music enhanced the words. By ignoring it, Meghan had rendered herself incognizant of the song's fullness.

Now a new fear loomed before her, one that suggested she had made a costly mistake.

What had she abandoned years earlier?

Would she be standing here right now if ...

The music stopped. Christine's body went limp, her eyes pinned to the instrument in a blank stare. "Wow," she said. "I wish someone loved me enough to write a song like that."

Her words prompted no response from Meghan, who continued to ponder in silence. The melody lingered in her mind, its rhythm waves of water, still in motion.

Finally, Christine asked, "Who *is* this guy?"

With her first syllable, Meghan found herself groggy from weeping. She brushed aside a meandering tear, cleared her voice, and tried to respond again. "He's a friend from outside Cleveland. I've known him my whole life."

"And he sent you a song like this out of the blue?"

Meghan's eyes felt swollen. "We were close. When he left for college, we kept in touch through the mail. He would send me song lyrics with a lot of his letters, and this was one of them. This was the only time he included music with it, though."

"This isn't just any song. He poured himself into it."

Frozen in shock, Meghan suppressed an onslaught of regret. "I've seen him make up amazing songs on the spot about nothing in particular. This could be one of those." But in her heart, Meghan knew better.

"Not this one. Too deep," Christine said. She spun around to face Meghan. "This guy loved you."

Meghan's gut sickened. "Yes, that's what he wrote in the letter that came with it." surrendered Meghan. She released a heavy exhale. "I didn't realize what I had with him. How I managed to overlook it is beyond me, because it's pretty clear right now." Sinking onto a chair, Meghan cocked her head against her palm.

"Danny ..."

anny tried to formulate a plan as he pulled in front of the Hartings' home. The southern Ohio sky released steady drops of rain that pelted his car. He had left his window cracked open since departing I-71. While he detected faint thunder in the distance, he saw no hint of lightning.

Yet the weather was the remotest topic from his mind.

Immediately Danny had rushed to Oxford upon hearing the news. Meghan needed him. He hadn't paused to explain to his parents where he was going. He hadn't considered how he would justify tomorrow's absence from school. By mere impulse, or perhaps instinct, Danny had climbed into his car and started to drive.

Dashing from his car to the Hartings' front porch, he tried to dodge the onslaught of water pellets, but they seeped into his shirt anyway. Danny knocked on the front door as he shook excess moisture from his arms. From the foyer on the other side of the door, he heard footsteps approach across the hardwood floor.

When she saw who the visitor was, Beth Harting forced a smile of compassion upon her otherwise downcast face. "A part of me knew you'd come, Danny."

"How's she doing, Beth?"

"Devastated. The news crushed her."

Danny tilted his head back and sighed. He could only imagine.

"She stayed here last night," Beth said. She brushed her hand against Danny's wet hair and her countenance lifted a bit. "Aren't you going to miss school by coming here?"

"I've only got a few weeks left," he said. "Besides, some things are more important."

Beth nodded. "She'll be glad to see you. I think she's in the woods. Would you like to come inside?"

"No thanks, I don't want to get your carpet wet. I'll walk around back and find her. Good to see you."

A brief wave over his shoulder, then Danny jogged around the house and crossed the back yard. When he reached the woods, he finagled past the familiar tree limbs, which hung low in an eerie sulk as the rain batted them down. As he approached the semi-bare patch where he and Meghan had camped almost a year earlier, he noticed a stark contrast. This time around, Danny halted when he saw her.

Meghan sat on a small patch of grass, her back toward him, and hadn't heard him coming. Queasy, Danny felt like someone had plowed a clenched fist into his belly.

With slow, cautious steps, he sauntered to her side but hesitated to sit. His heart broke for her. Meghan must have heard the patter of rain on his shoes as he stood behind her, because she turned and looked up at him. Even from several feet away, Danny could see her eyes were swollen red from continual tears. Fragile as silk, Danny had never seen her as vulnerable as she now appeared. Regardless of the circumstance, Meghan had always emanated strength unaware.

But not today.

Danny sat down and wrapped his arm around her. Meghan spoke nothing, but soon she buried her head in his chest and sobbed. Though the trees provided considerable shelter, the rain had drenched her nonetheless. The surrounding patches of dirt, now thickened into mud, had splashed and smeared over her pant legs. She must have sat there for an hour.

Danny examined her wet hair and delicate body. At first, he wanted to kiss her. The next instant, however, Danny felt a horrid sense of guilt as he beheld the sight of Meghan in evident pain.

Wrapping his other arm around her, he rocked her gently, cradled her as if protecting a child from impending harm. How he wished he could endure the agony on her behalf. Torn as he was, Danny knew what he experienced was a mere fraction of what pierced Meghan's heart.

After a long lull void of words, Meghan broke the silence.

"It seemed so real," she said, her voice scratchy and weak. "For that brief period of time, everything was coming together. It was supposed to be a brand new chance, my opportunity to *give*." As though in search of mercy, Meghan peered at the relentless sky, which answered her with nothing but more rain. "It would have been easier if I had never known about the baby than to know I was pregnant and make the plans, only to have them ripped apart."

Danny stared at her. It was all he could muster, aware of his inadequacy to comfort her. For that matter, he doubted there were words sufficient to alleviate her distress.

Meghan bathed her words in a throaty, almost inaudible, groan. "I feel numb, like a part of me died with the baby."

Danny tried to maintain control, but he could feel his eyes widen with fear against his will. Still, he listened.

Scared, he listened closely.

Minutes crawled before Meghan spoke again. Her tears mixed with raindrops and fell to her mouth as a courageous smile twitched at the corner of her mouth. "They say when you first feel the baby inside, it's like a butterfly. Did you know that?"

Danny shook his head, tears welling up in his own eyes. He fended them off and forced a smile instead.

"I still had a few more weeks to go before I would have felt anything," Meghan continued. "So when everything seemed still, it never occurred to me that the baby wasn't alive." She shook her head. "I never even knew what those were like, the butterfly flutters."

Danny rubbed her arm. The April moisture felt arm upon her sleeves.

"Last week, I started getting cramps. They just stayed with me, except they got worse and worse every day. Something about it struck me as odd, so yesterday, I called the OB-GYN and went in for an appointment," she said, her lips crumpling. "It started out like any other appointment. The assistant was in good humor when she came into the room to do the ultrasound, just like always. She joked around a little, broke the ice."

Wiping her tears, Meghan sniffled.

"The assistant steered the device around, and the images were on screen. I was still uncomfortable from the cramps, but it was worth it, knowing a baby would come along in a matter of months. So I relaxed. Watched. Listened."

Meghan paused, and Danny detected terror in her eyes. "Then I realized I didn't hear a heartbeat. I heard the noise from the machine and the printer, but I didn't hear my little baby. That's when I looked over at the assistant, but she wouldn't look at me. She stared straight at the screen. That's when I leaned in for a closer look and saw no movement. The assistant stayed calm, said the doctor would be in shortly, then walked out. So there I was, staring at the screen while she left the room. As I got dressed, thoughts started racing through my head: Did they forget to turn up the sound? Why wasn't the assistant smiling when she left? And why was my baby just floating there? I started getting nervous and really hot. I just sat in that dark room with the cold computer light coming from the screen and an image of my baby frozen in place."

Nausea settled into Danny's stomach. He attempted to hide it, constricting his muscles, hoping Meghan couldn't feel them as they tightened.

"Finally, the doctor walked into the room, looked over the printouts, and checked the screen. And that's when she broke the news to me." Meghan's lower lip quivered, her voice cracking between sobs. "She told me I had lost the baby. I just sat there stunned. My mind was a total blank, like a beige wall. I couldn't even—" She threw up her hands, at a clear loss for words. "It was beyond comprehension. So I asked her, 'How did this happen? Did I do something to make the little baby die?'"

Danny cringed. His heart wrenched.

"And she told me, 'No, these things sometimes happen,' then went through the medical explanation, telling me it was beyond my control. But all I heard were these muffled noises from her, because it was a major blow to me. I mean, what else do you do at that point? What do you say?" Defenseless, Meghan appeared to surrender with a halfhearted shrug, her voice diminishing to

126 126 John Herrick

a whisper. "She said she was sorry. So there was my baby on the screen, the last image that had been recorded, the last picture I ever got to see." Meghan stared ahead. "I asked her if she knew the baby's gender, and she said it was a little boy."

Danny closed his eyes.

"I drove home shocked," Meghan said. "Went to the pantry to start making dinner, but I couldn't do it. Instead, I stumbled to the kitchen table and sat down. And at that point, it dawned on me that there had been a living person inside my body, and he had died." With a laborious exhale, she appeared to surrender to grief. "I need to go in tomorrow for something they call a 'D and C.' They're going to scrape the poor, helpless baby out, then it'll be as if nothing ever happened. They'll go on with their lives, and I get to go on with mine." With a quiet grunt, Meghan said, "Oh, it makes me sick to my stomach to think about it."

Meghan cradled her knees. As he watched her, Danny could only imagine the images that must have flashed through Meghan's mind. Those images had probably repeated countless times in the last twenty-four hours. She shook her head and closed her eyes but couldn't seem to escape the grueling onslaught of pain. "I know it must have been my fault—something I did, something I didn't do. And this time, I finally hurt someone else."

Danny held her tighter, rocked her with slower, broader sways. "No, Meg. That's not true."

"I picked up a bag of heavy groceries at the store, with cans of vegetables in it. It could've been caused by stress from that."

Unable to hold them back any longer, Danny yielded to the tears as they started to roll down his face. "No, Meg ..." Angry with himself, he wanted to remain strong for her, but his bones were shaking inside.

Her eyes widening, Meghan looked worried. "You know, there was that one time when I was sixteen—"

Danny grew urgent. "Meghan, stop. Don't go there. That was years ago. It has nothing to do with this."

Meghan pressed her head harder into Danny's chest. "I want to tell the little baby, 'I'm so sorry.'" She sobbed. "'I'm so sorry your mommy failed you, little baby ...'"

"Shh ..."

As Danny held her tighter, Meghan curled her legs close, as though to trade places with the infant she had seen on a monitor but had never touched.

CHAPTER 15
JUNE 2007

His determination was solid. Danny darted inside his house and locked the door. He raced to the telephone and yanked its cord from the wall jack, wasting no time to stop in his tracks. Then, grabbing his guitar on the way, he dashed to the kitchen and sat down at the table, where his notebook already awaited him. Guitar in his lap, Danny began to strum it in a feverish attack.

To reach Meghan's heart, Danny knew his only mechanism was the one that had touched her heart in the past: a song. Despite the altered circumstances that might have arisen during their time apart, Danny was confident her heart had remained unchanged. No one else had ever known who she truly was on the inside. Danny alone had seen the vulnerability she hid beneath her firm exterior.

He was created for her.

Danny now battled for his destiny. This would be his final opportunity to win Meghan back. While aware that he could lose this fight in the end, his conscience would never rest until he had exhausted this, his most extreme option.

The fever burned.

Danny contended neither against Brian nor against the past. Rather, he battled against the status quo. Against the reasoning that suggested he was too late. Against the impenetrable wall that masked his future.

Against the hollow crater in his soul that would remain empty without the only girl he had ever loved.

The fever burned.

His writer's block, once a giant, dissolved before him now. While the task at hand proved a challenge, words flowed out of him. Years spent longing for Meghan and the resulting emptiness, once pent up within him, broke forth in a torrent like a river overpowering a mighty levy. Danny reached for phrases like desperate gasps for air. Indeed, for Danny, the resulting song would symbolize his survival, for a part of him would die without Meghan. Danny felt small beads of perspiration aggregate on his brow.

The fever burned.

Strange enough, he found the current situation similar to when he composed "Meghan's Song" years ago. This time, however, he perceived a mounting urgency. Taking nothing for granted, Danny experimented with concepts, events and emotions that had consolidated to form the man he was today.

Danny manipulated rhymes, tested major and minor chords. He had transformed into an insatiable perfectionist, for a critical truth resounded within him: The final outcome must exceed perfection. It must be his masterpiece. Settling for less would risk losing everything.

In a matter of minutes, Danny grappled with fresh bursts of joy, despondency, purpose and fear. When coupled with his long-term suppression of internal angst, Danny's resolve, an anchor of emotion, strapped itself to him.

And in a sudden, unanticipated development, Danny wept.

At last, he severed his eyes from the project and forced himself from the chair. According to the clock on the wall, more than four hours had passed since he'd first isolated himself inside the house. Danny needed a cigarette.

Leaving the porch light off, he walked out the back door into the darkness, into the roar of ocean waves that pounded against the shore. And pounded. And pounded.

The humid breeze cooled his cheeks, which stung from the tears that had dried and tightened against his skin.

Slapping the pack against his palm, he removed a cigarette and lit it in the dark. Its embers glowed a hot orange as they fell to the ground.

A few drafts and Danny felt himself drawn back into the house. He extinguished the cigarette nearly whole to return to the project that compelled him.

As he glanced at the slew of creative impulses that had manifested on paper, Danny sensed a song title emerge: "Breathing Yesterday."

CHAPTER 16
JUNE 2007

The aroma of fresh-brewed coffee invigorated Danny's senses. Through a small kitchen window, he peered across the vast array of water and absorbed the initial glow of dawn as it spread upward from behind the ocean.

Pouring himself a cup, he decided to drink the coffee black. Danny's eyes felt bloodshot and heavy, as if each had gained a pound. Shortly past midnight he'd decided to ignore the clock and, as a result, had worked through the night. Satisfied in the end, Danny had completed "Breathing Yesterday" and cleared the kitchen table a few minutes ago.

After brief deliberation, Danny realized that he could not squeeze out another emotional release. Forthright and factual, his letter would give Meghan a background on his current status and explain his reason for contacting her. The song would explain the rest.

On his way to the table, he gulped his coffee, which burned his throat on its way down. He sat on the opposite side from where he had composed Meghan's new song, grabbed a blank sheet of paper, and found the words waiting at his fingertips:

Meg,

It's been quite a while, hasn't it? Hopefully I'm reaching you at your current address—it was the latest one I had.

Coming from out of nowhere, this letter has probably blown you away, so please let me explain: I've done a lot of personal searching lately, especially the last few months, and have evaluated everything—the past, the present, and the future. Much of who I am today I owe to you. The friendship and unique bond that we shared have changed my world. Though we haven't kept in touch, your impact endures. My life is better because you were part of it.

For that reason, I had to write this letter and compose a final song for you called "Breathing Yesterday." (Wow—how long has it been since you've read one of those!) I felt that we left a few loose ends and needed to do what I could to bring about some closure. And as you know, I seem to communicate best through music.

Life is good here. As you know, I've lived at Sunset Beach, South Carolina, for several years. As an indirect result of your past encouragement, I sing weekends at McGrady's Bar & Grill. It's located at Destiny Landing (we call it "The Landing" around here), a tourist attraction off of Gateway Boulevard. Right outside the restaurant is a footbridge that crosses over a small lake. Many times, I've stood on The Landing's bridge during breaks, looked out over the water, and wondered about you and your life. So in a way, you could say that this song was born there.

I hope all is well with you. Meghan, I realize—and

respect—that you're with Brian now. Please know I ask nothing in return, other than for you to allow "Breathing Yesterday" to speak to your heart. I'm always here for you and believe destiny, whatever shape it may take, will win in the end.

Take care, Meg. I think of you often. I've always loved you, and without a doubt, a piece of me always will. You're a special woman—more so than you realize.

Thanks for everything.

Love always,
Danny
P.S. If you ever need me, you can reach my cell phone at 843-555-4219. My address is on the envelope.

As he read through the text again, Danny was pleased with how much less time the letter had required versus the labor he had poured into "Breathing Yesterday." Comfortable with the content of both, he prepared a large manila envelope with Meghan's address. After a quick trip to make a photocopy of Meghan's new song, he would deposit it at the post office.

But he would do that later. Exhausted, his tar-colored coffee powerless against a sleep-deprived night, a sluggish Danny Bale dragged himself away from the kitchen and crawled into bed. Chilled by the morning air, he pulled a sheet to his chin and fell asleep without effort.

• • •

Danny entered the post office around noon and found the counter short-staffed. Tailing the long line, he considered returning at a less busy time but quashed the idea immediately. He had already discovered the personal cost of allowing Meghan to fade from his life and balked at the idea of losing one more hour. He was determined to include his packet in that day's outgoing mail.

Eyeing the anonymous folks who stood between the nylon tape of waist-high poles, Danny wondered what their packages contained. Patting a comb-over hairstyle, a tall man in a dark suit and tie held what looked like a package of business documents. A pudgy woman shifted a box from one arm to the other. Bulky, but apparently lightweight, Danny guessed her box a birthday gift with a stuffed animal inside.

Glancing at his own envelope by comparison, Danny became acute to the broader, more significant ramifications his own mailing contained. Greater than a business transaction and more notable than an extra candle on a birthday cake, Danny realized his entire future might hinge on the item in his grip. He pressed the envelope against his thigh and read the menu of price options that hung overhead. Nervous, his stomach rippled.

Upon reaching the counter, a male postal worker with a curious blond ponytail greeted him.

Business casual, Danny mused. How times had changed since Danny's own corporate tenure.

"How would you like to send this?" asked the worker, his face exuding nonchalance as he flipped the envelope over, examining both sides for irregularities.

"First class is fine." Danny wished he could afford to overnight it.

"Do you need a delivery confirmation?"

"No, thanks."

Ponytail flung the envelope on the electric scale and punched away at his computer. "First-class package from Sunset Beach to Oxford, Ohio, should arrive in two to three business days."

Nodding his approval, Danny pulled cash from his wallet and paid the worker, who printed a postage label and slapped it to the envelope's corner. As he observed the postal worker's routine attitude, rubber stamping the piece of mail for official good measure, Danny marveled. Danny's own destiny was, for this man, a passing moment, insignificant and mundane. Indeed, it struck Danny that each manifestation of destiny is detectable only by those whose hearts are connected to it.

After thanking the worker, Danny walked away, peering over his shoulder to watch the man toss the envelope into a white collection bin along with the rest of the outgoing mail, one piece of hundreds.

As he stepped out the door, Danny heard Ponytail's voice bellow from behind.

"Next!"

CHAPTER 17
JUNE 2007

Meghan found her mother perusing the menu when she entered The Hen's Nest, a restaurant in Hamilton, a community near Oxford.

Meghan always enjoyed seeing her mother dressed in business attire when they met for lunch: skirt suit, fashionable eyeglasses, graying hair pulled into a taut ponytail. Beth worked at a bank around the corner, where she had spent the last eight years. Though she never verbalized it, often Meghan noted the difference between her own casual apparel and her mother's professional appearance, a reminder of the potential that existed if her own college career ever concluded.

Mother and daughter exchanged kisses on the cheek. Although just the two of them would meet, the hostess had pampered them with a table for four against the front window. Placing her purse on the seat beside her, Meghan sat down and took a quick glance at High Street, where a series of cars splashed through puddles as a summer shower fell.

"Have you waited long?" asked Meghan.

"No, honey. In fact, the waitress hasn't checked back yet."

Meghan dropped a lemon slice into her water glass as she

scanned a menu of omelets, salads, and light sandwiches. With a closing time at two o'clock in the afternoon, The Hen's Nest catered to Hamilton's business district with its slew of breakfast and brunch specialties.

"I can't decide," Beth said. "What looks good to you?"

"I think I'm gonna go with a Caesar salad."

"A salad sounds good. I don't need any extra weight anyway."

Meghan sighed as she examined her mother's tighter-than-average figure. "Mom, you don't need to watch your weight."

"I want to look good for your dad next month. Guiltless Asian chicken salad it is!" Beth folded the menu.

Meghan sat up straight. "Why? Are you and Dad going somewhere?"

"I twisted his arm into a getaway for our anniversary weekend."

"That should be fun for you two. What's the plan?"

"A weekend at the Hilton in Cincinnati. Dinner and a play one night, a baseball game the next night—you know, for him." Beth winked.

On occasion, Travis and Beth Harting had peppered their marriage with romantic weekend interludes at nearby destinations, and though Meghan couldn't pinpoint why, she took pleasure in hearing about their middle-aged escapades. During childhood, Meghan had pictured herself in a marriage resembling theirs, but whose getaway locations were far more exotic—weekends spent relaxing in gondolas on Italian canals. Nowadays, however, Meghan found herself willing to settle for a bottle of wine and a few days at an Oxford hotel, but Brian, in workaholic fashion, refused to sacrifice the time.

Jerking herself back to the reality of The Hen's Nest and the scents of croissants and bacon upon the air, Meghan placed her napkin on her lap. "I don't think you ever told me about you and Dad before you were married. You've mentioned meeting in college and your first date, but not much beyond that."

Leaning forward to rest on her hand, Beth's eyes seemed to become effervescent, as though brightening at memories unforgotten but overdue for a revisit. "I could tell he was interested in me before he ever asked me out. And I'll bet I never told you about the time he scaled the wall at my dorm when we were nineteen."

"Are you kidding? How high?"

"I was on the third floor in the corner room, and there was lattice up the sides of the building with ivy growing along it. Well, one night around midnight, when we were still friends, I heard someone whisper my name down below. At first I ignored it, but it didn't stop—'Beth! Hey Beth!' Finally, I walked over to the window and looked out. There was your dad, standing in the lawn with his hands cupped around his mouth. And you wouldn't picture him doing this, but he started climbing up the lattice, just to make me laugh. Actually, that was his reason when he started to climb. After he got past the first floor, I have a hunch his male ego kicked in, so he kept on climbing."

"And he made it all the way?"

"Not quite," Beth chuckled. "The lattice began to crack, but he was too high up to back down, so he scrambled to get up to my window and jump inside. But the harder he worked, the more of a mess he made, because the lattice began to fall apart! I watched pieces of white wood fall to the ground and was frightened your dad would be next. Sure enough, the lattice gave way and sent him in a freefall into the shrubbery."

"No! Was he all right?"

"He was so humiliated—and a bit shaken up. There he was,

trying his best to impress a girl with his chivalry, and the poor guy landed on his butt. I'm sure he was bright red."

"On which end?"

"Funny. His face, probably. I'm sure the other end was more of a black and blue! Then, as if his fall wasn't enough, he saw a flashlight whirl around outside, an RA trying to figure out what had caused the racket. So, your dad hobbled away with a limp. He never got caught, though. Just a little bruised up." Giggling, Beth shook her head. "To this day, I don't know what possessed him to do it."

Meghan leaned forward. "I can't picture Dad scaling a wall like that! It's a good thing he didn't break his leg. Did he ever regret doing it?"

Tongue in cheek, Beth sipped her water. "He got the girl in the end."

"Were you interested in him beyond friendship back then?"

"The idea had never crossed my mind. We got along together well. Needless to say, he was comfortable around me to the point of making a fool of himself. But he was still Travis Harting, the guy I always beat at the pool table."

"You ended up marrying him, though."

In mocked apathy, Beth shrugged. "He grew on me." She lifted her glass to take another sip but stopped short and added, "And I *still* beat him at pool. Some things never change."

The imagery of her father's gravitational challenge frolicking in her mind, Meghan decided on a glass of raspberry tea as the waitress arrived. After apologizing for the delay, the waitress collected their orders and hurried away, grabbing their menus in the process. From the woman's demeanor, Meghan guessed that she was a single mother trying to make ends meet.

Meghan felt Beth scrutinize her the way mothers do.

Beth asked, "Has Brian eased up on the marriage idea?"

Meghan rubbed a fake knot at the back of her neck as she eased against the back of her chair.

"I'm sorry, honey," Beth said. "I wasn't trying to pry."

Besides Danny, her mother was perhaps the only person Meghan trusted with confidential discussions. By habit, after her pregnancy, when a handful of her most personal secrets became the topic of gossip among friends, Meghan proffered few details to anyone. She now preferred a guarded approach. Meghan blamed her own poor judgment for the pain of betrayal and had vowed never to be hurt in such a manner twice.

In an even tone, Meghan replied, "You've never pried, Mom." Meghan watched a drop of condensation as it zigzagged down her glass and soaked into the pastel, woven tablecloth. "Brian and I are in our thirties and not getting any younger. It's frustrating to be in a relationship with a person who's content with minimal commitment." Baffled, she shook her head. "Apparently he believes I'll stay with him regardless."

"Is he aware you feel this way?"

"I've mentioned it here and there, woven it into conversations so he won't think I'm trying to pressure him. Early on, I tried to have actual discussions about marriage, but after a few of those, he refused to talk about it further."

"Are *you* still considering marriage?"

Pausing, Meghan found the question a rough pill to swallow. She knew her mother paid as much attention to her bodily nuances as to her words. As a child, this skill had rendered futile many of Meghan's attempts to hide pertinent information. In her adulthood, however, she found her mother's prowess to be a valuable asset while navigating through assorted dilemmas. Either way, though, Meghan found it painstaking as it cut to the core of her pride. "I don't know," she admitted. "I *thought* that was what I wanted."

"Has something changed?"

Meghan pondered the question. Unable to provide a direct answer, she stalled by asking, "Mom, while you and Dad were engaged and the months passed, did you ever have a nagging curiosity that you settled?" Before Beth could respond, Meghan wanted to retract her question. "Never mind," she said, stammering as she spoke. "That's a dumb thing to ask."

Beth studied her daughter's visage. "Do you think you settled for Brian?"

"Our relationship has grown ... comfortable, almost like a habit." Although she couldn't identify where it occurred, the conversation's obstacles had dissolved, leaving Meghan's heart naked as it lay on the table. Relieved, she couldn't recall when she had last spoken with such candor. "Oftentimes, I'll get real still in bed after he's asleep and wonder how I allowed myself to become ..." Her voice trailed.

"What, honey?"

"Dependent." Meghan locked eyes with Beth.

"To the point that I'm bound—whether he wants me around or not." Astonished, Meghan remarked, "Isn't that strange? It's not like we *need* each other. I got by fine before he came along, and we don't own anything significant together today. I mean, he wanted a house, so he bought it himself. We don't even own a dog together."

Beth squinted, watching her daughter fidget with her hands. "Maybe you need to think back to how your relationship began. What attracted you to him at first?"

"All I can say is that it grew naturally. I was opposed to a relationship at first, remember?"

"All right. But if you needed to put your finger on a single detail about Brian, what would it be?"

Meghan fiddled with her fork, using the prongs as an axis and pivoting the handle from side to side. "This is going to sound awful," she said, "but I think it was *fear*."

Beth cocked her head and raised her eyebrows.

Now Meghan couldn't bear to look her mother in the eyes. "Fear of ending up alone," she added.

"Meghan, you were in your twenties. Why would you have been afraid of that?"

Ashamed, Meghan bit her lip as she relived her past. Her exhale hot within her nostrils, she mustered the courage to admit the key sentiment that had tormented her for years: "Guys don't want a girl who's been knocked up, Mom."

Beth offered no reply.

Meghan could feel her stomach knotting. She had long considered her statement as true, and it felt like needle pricks to her heart. A strong-willed woman, Meghan applied rigorous standards not only to others, but also to herself. In the hidden corners of her conscience rested a continual regret, an inability to forgive herself for mistakes that lay strewn in her past, though she craved such forgiveness.

The stressed waitress returned to the table with their orders, asked if she could bring anything else, then smiled and hurried away. Not before Meghan caught a quick glimpse of the woman's tired eyes, however. Despite the requisite smile, Meghan identified with the downcast X-factor that lurked behind the surface of the woman's irises.

Famished, Meghan and Beth dug into their salads. Catching the faint scent of Beth's Asian dressing, Meghan noticed her mother appeared engrossed in thought, the subject of which reached beyond locating her next bite.

Judging from the creases on her mother's forehead, Meghan figured her pregnancy remark had stricken her mother as odd. Holding her fork inches from her mouth, Beth said, "It seems to me that you weren't alone back then, Meghan. Wasn't Danny there for you?"

Meghan couldn't help but grin at the comment. She interlaced her fingers and rested her chin on them. "Yeah, he was." Her eyes sparkled as memories danced. Setting her fork on the plate, her hands animated, Meghan leaned forward. "Did you know he sent me a baby package in the mail when he found out I was pregnant? Homemade, not one of those gift sets. Oh, Mom, it was so cute! A one-piece sleeper, burping pads, a bottle of baby bath—all the details. It was obvious he'd put a lot of planning into it."

Falling back against her chair, Meghan crossed her arms as she dug for more treasures in her mind. Beth looked on at Meghan's surge of spontaneity.

All of a sudden, the memories made Meghan feel as special as when Danny's actions had originally occurred. Her lingering smile began a slow fade into rich subtlety as her arms went limp. Though mentally miles away from The Hen's Nest, she disclosed, "He told me he would marry me and adopt the baby if it would help."

Beth attempted—a millisecond too late—to gloss over the widening of her eyes. Meghan caught a glimpse. Meghan had shared numerous secrets with her mother, but Danny's informal proposal had not been one of them.

Beth remained silent at the revelation. Meghan eyed the tiny bump in the corner of her mother's cheek, where Beth had lodged her tongue.

In a poor attempt to feign casualness, Beth asked, "Have you, uh, heard from Danny lately?"

"We haven't talked in years. Not since he was in college. Does his mom ever mention how he's doing?"

"According to Lori, he's still living down at the beach. They don't get to see him often. He rarely comes home."

"That's odd, considering how close his family is. Has she ever said why?"

"He won't tell her, and she can't fathom why. His departure seemed sudden and uncalculated, so she believes his reason goes beyond a love for the ocean."

Meghan grinned. "Artists."

"I suppose." With one eyebrow raised, Beth examined her daughter as she brushed aside some excess dressing from a lettuce leaf. "Do you ever notice how you shift gears when you talk about Danny?"

That was one question Meghan had not anticipated. "What do you mean? My face changes?"

"Your whole demeanor changes. You become more vibrant. You talk faster. And your eyes gleam."

"Danny's a great guy."

"You two were certainly good friends. I think you provided each other with a lot of support over the years."

"He made me believe there was more to me than anyone else could see."

"That's a special quality, babe."

"There were times when Danny would look into my eyes, and I could've sworn he saw right through them, like a laser. But it wasn't harsh; it was tender. He made me feel like a princess whenever he did that."

"How did you lose touch with each other?"

Meghan shrugged. "I suppose our lives just got busy. I got caught up in mine; he got caught up in his. Before you know it, the years pass and you're immersed in a different routine. Friends don't always remain as close as you and Lori do."

"Do you ever think of him?"

"I do miss him on occasion," Meghan admitted.

Beth paused again. "Honey, I realize I'm your mother, and you may not want to hear all this from me ..."

Meghan watched as her mother took another bite and swallowed. It appeared Beth now took her turn at avoiding eye contact. "Are you sure there wasn't more than friendship between you and Danny?"

"What makes you say that?"

"Well, you told me he offered to marry you when the baby was coming. Most friends wouldn't go to that extreme."

This hadn't occurred to Meghan before. Granted, she had always considered Danny unique. Even as teenagers, an unusual quality had resonated from him, one that distinguished him from any other guy she had known. But because the offer of marriage had fit Danny's character so well, she had failed to perceive it beyond face value.

"Actually," Meghan said, "he was in love with me at one point."

"The two of you sure kept your secrets quite well. I never heard about that one."

"He wrote it in a letter once. We kept in touch that way his whole time in college, writing letters back and forth. Then, out of nowhere, he sent me something he had written called 'Meghan's Song.' It was late September—I'll never forget it. He'd sent me lyrics all along for different songs, but in this case, he included the music with it. I read through the lyrics, and they were beautiful." A shiver raced up Meghan's spine. "Ooh, it touched me. In the letter that accompanied the song, he admitted that he loved me and explained that 'Meghan's Song' was an outgrowth of that."

"Did you love *him*?"

Meghan felt the penetration of her mother's eyes. She jabbed at her lettuce before she finally said, "Mom, I'm scared I broke his heart. I was involved with Brian at that point and was determined to make that relationship work. I felt so weak and couldn't bring myself into a long-distance relationship. Danny was hundreds of miles away at school, and I needed stability in my life. I needed to succeed at *something*."

"All of those details aside, did you love Danny?"

Meghan shook her head. "Mom, I would have ended up hurting him, and he didn't deserve that."

"But did you *love* him?" Persistent, Beth asked the question in a near whisper.

At last, Meghan laid her fork on the plate, dabbed her mouth with her napkin. In a quiet surrender, she said, "Yes, I did."

Beth smirked and continued to poke at her salad.

When Beth didn't reply, Meghan added, "But I thought I loved Brian, too. So which is true?"

"Listen to your heart, Meghan. If you love him, you *know* it." Beth swallowed a tiny mandarin orange. "Besides, you can't run away from it. It'll continue to tug on you."

"Does it really matter at this point, Mom? Danny has his own life now. He drove to the Carolinas."

A glint of insight in her eyes, Beth pointed her fork toward her daughter. "Call me a mother," she said, "but I don't think he drove to the beach." Beth swallowed another bite. "I think he *ran*."

CHAPTER 18
SEPTEMBER 22, 2000

In spite of the sunshine that bathed the building's exterior, Danny Bale's room carried the same musty dimness as the rest of the college dormitory. With a bored yawn, Danny finished reading a chapter for a business management class. He slammed the textbook shut, shoved it onto a shelf, and lounged back in his chair. The smooth, gray floor tiles felt cold and dusty against the soles of his feet.

From the hallway, he could hear his neighbor practicing on—and falling from—a unicycle, preparing to don the mascot costume for Saturday's football game. Snickering at that idea, Danny padded over to his window and watched as a small group of coeds strolled below. Had he not fallen behind in his reading, Danny would be outside as well.

One glance toward Meghan's latest letter at the corner of his desk, and Danny livened up. She still awaited a reply. With a jolt of fresh energy, he sat back down and pulled a set of sheet music from his desk drawer. Giving the arrangement a final perusal, he nodded to himself and ripped out a sheet of notebook paper.

He was hesitant to compose his letter, already aware that

words would fail to suffice. Although they burned within him, drawing them to the surface would prove a challenge. Nevertheless, he put his pen to paper in blind fashion, the same way he would approach a new song:

> Meg,
>
> Hey! How's your week? I'm A-OK here. Just finished playing catch-up on some homework for my management class. I've got an exam on it next week, which is gonna be a killer! But this college thing will be over soon. Yep, I'll have a full-time job with a steady income—no more of this impoverished student life! Hey, what do you say we chip in together on a condo in Malibu, and I'll get a job out there? Just kidding.
>
> So how did things go between you and Brian the other day? When you wrote last time, you mentioned you were going to have a talk about where the relationship was headed. Did that ever happen? I have to say, I don't think you know what a great girl you are. You deserve the best. Don't you dare settle for less.
>
> It's funny that you asked how the songwriting's been coming along. The reason I haven't sent any lyrics with my recent letters is because I've been focusing on one particular song, which I've enclosed. It's entitled, "Meghan's Song," and it addresses some things I've had on my heart for a while now.
>
> As our friendship grew through the years, I found myself seeking to know you better—not merely as a friend, but from a place deeper within me. And the more familiar I became with you, the further I wanted to search.

Throughout the process of writing "Meghan's Song," as well as in the weeks that preceded it, I weighed all the factors that have come into play between us. I found myself arriving at a single conclusion, one I've known inside for years but, for some reason, has taken this long for me to recognize: I've fallen in love with you, Meg.

At this point, Danny grew nervous as he wondered what would travel through Meghan's mind when she read this profession of love. In fact, this marked the first time he had ever verbalized such words to anyone. Would the notion touch her heart? Maybe it would frighten her. Perhaps she would never want to speak to him again. All of a sudden, the risk seemed to double for Danny. His pulse raced as he continued to write:

To most people, this would sound ridiculous since you and I never dated, but it stems from how close we became over the course of time.

You probably don't remember this, but there was one day in particular, a couple years back, right after you discovered you were pregnant. Your dad and I had finished moving you into your new apartment, and when he left for lunch, you and I sat and talked about your becoming a mom, as well as the stigmatism you'd faced with your old friends. I can still remember how excited you were as you described the future—your eyes were so radiant. You seemed to bear your soul to me. Unlike the solid exterior you usually display, I had the privilege of glimpsing a side of you that I'd never seen before. You allowed me to see who you truly are on the inside, and I fell in love with that girl I saw. It was different from the physical attraction I felt the night we slept in the woods beneath the stars. This time, as we sat in your apartment, a resolve built within me that drew me nearer to you. Yet, at the same time, my heart melted for you. And now, as I look back on that day and on the years in which we grew closer, I realize you're the only person I want to spend my life with. I love you, and "Meghan's Song" is my attempt to put that affection into a form that will reach the deeper part of you—the part I fell in love with.

I've also enclosed the sheet music. I know you don't play an instrument, but it seemed you would only have half the picture without it, and that would do your song an injustice.

I apologize, because this must be awkward for you. I don't know how it fits into the situation between you and Brian. But when the revelation hit me, I needed to wrap words around it. Unlike many songs from the past that were written about no one specific, this one comes directly from my soul.

I hope to hear from you soon, but please don't feel pressured to rush into a reply. I'll wait as long as you need.

With all my heart,
Danny

Well, here goes, he thought. *I can't believe I'm actually doing this.*

CHAPTER 19
JUNE 2007

Meghan pulled her red Honda into the garage, right beside Brian's BMW. Removing her sunglasses as she walked down to the curb, she could smell the driveway asphalt, which blistered as it roasted beneath the sun.

Emptying the contents from the mailbox, she noticed a large, manila envelope, bent in half to fit inside the box and wrapped around the rest of the day's mail.

As she made her way back to the garage, Meghan flipped through the usual assortment of bills and fliers, including a weekly advertisement that flaunted a special telephone rate. She hated those. After responding to one of the company's hooks in the past, the customer service representative had informed her that the prices were not valid in her area. Now irritated by the continued annoyance, she ripped the ad into tiny pieces—a feat of smug defiance, one that caused several other mailings to slide from her grip and fall to the ground.

Retrieving the fugitive pieces of mail and brushing them clean, Meghan grew curious about the manila envelope that had enclosed them so feebly. Her eyes caught the Sunset Beach, South Carolina, postmark location first, then darted to the return address, in which Danny Bale's name stood prominent in black permanent marker.

That's bizarre, Meghan thought. She stopped in her tracks and grinned. Shaking the envelope, she found it to be light-weight, a handful of papers inside. Puzzled, the packet reminded her of one she had received back when Danny was in college. The one in which he'd enclosed "Meghan's Song," along with a letter that had shocked her with a declaration of love.

What would Danny have sent her after all this time?

Meghan took a leisurely stride through the garage. She examined the envelope's exterior, more inquisitive of its contents with each passing moment. She hadn't heard from Danny Bale since … well, she couldn't remember. A slew of spontaneous thoughts sprung forth: *I had just wondered how he's doing. Why would he decide to write out of nowhere? No way, surely Mom didn't call him—at least, I hope not!*

When she reached the door to the house, Meghan pulled out her keys, eager to read the letter as soon as she got inside. But as she touched the lock, she stopped abruptly. She stared over her shoulder at Brian's silver BMW, glossy from a fresh wax, still clicking after a late-afternoon commute.

Slapping Danny's envelope against her palm, Meghan turned back and placed the mysterious item in the glove compartment of her Honda. She would need to read it later. She didn't know how Brian would respond if he knew she had received fresh correspondence from Danny, and they didn't need another argument to erupt.

Locking the car behind her, she walked into the house, mail in hand, one letter less.

CHAPTER 20
JUNE 2007

That evening, Meghan pulled into the driveway at her parents' house shortly after dinnertime. Though they lived in a residential neighborhood, each home rested on an acre lot. Travis and Beth Hartings' home sat at the far end of the street, where automobiles seldom passed and the environment was always silent.

Stepping out of her car, Meghan hid her purse beneath the driver's seat and grabbed Danny's manila envelope, still unopened a few hours after appearing in her mailbox.

Strolling up to the house, Meghan peered through a window on the garage door and, to her relief, discovered her parents were not home. Meghan was not in a conversational mood, and she didn't want to concoct an explanation for Danny's sudden correspondence while not even she herself knew why he'd written. The envelope had nipped at her curiosity all through dinner, to such an extent that Brian had inquired why she seemed so distracted.

Rounding the corner of the house, Meghan walked across the back lawn and into the woods. Brushing several branches aside, she came to the small clearing where she and Danny had once spent the night beneath the trees and stars, the spot where they had shared a sleeping bag as Danny composed a song with ad-hoc agility. She had visited the spot after that event, but the spot had seemed dead somehow. Now, a bittersweet pang, gentle yet abrupt, settled in her belly. The dirt ground and its surrounding foliage seemed all too familiar.

Meghan recalled something Danny had spoken here years earlier: *You know what's amazing to me? Those things we see in the sky have been there for thousands of years.* He had said it in reference to the stars above, their electric glow unmistakable but often taken for granted. Perhaps the bond she shared with Danny had fallen prey to the same trap.

Meghan sat on the ground and ran her finger along the envelope's seam, her hands in a tremble. If Danny had decided to break his silence and send a large, unexpected packet, it must be important. She wondered if a specific event had triggered his communication, or maybe a question had weighed on his mind for months. Meghan opened the envelope and removed a letter with sheet music attached. Familiarity compounded.

She rested her elbows on bent knees and started to read Danny's letter. By the time she finished the second paragraph, her eyes glided with precision across each line.

Another paragraph passed. And another.

When she finished reading the text, she felt a lump wedge itself in her throat, making it difficult to breathe. She pondered the letter a while, then looked over the music and lyrics. The melody seemed to dance along the staffs, and the chords appeared beautiful, their notes layered on top of each other. Still, Danny's lyrics had always touched her most.

"Breathing Yesterday."

Meghan was glad she had read the letter first. She thought it a pity to read the lyrics while ignorant of their significance.

She read through the song, page by page. Metaphors and mental images emerged, a common occurrence when reading his songs in the past, she remembered. Though forgotten as the years progressed, she reminisced on the intimacy of the experiences they had shared. Meghan was well acquainted with Danny's soul.

BREATHING YESTERDAY

There's something familiar about these shades of blue
I was standing at these crossroads a time ago
I find surfacing a welcome déjà vu
It's been way too long, too many years flying solo

In my mind I see a glowing in your eyes right now
The same old flicker I kept grasping as the days went by
Frail words could never justify how
The attempt would be futile, I can no longer deny

CHORUS:
I've found myself
Discontent in breathing yesterday
There's a ringing in my memory
I tried to hide away
And I'm diving down
To the depths of my heart
That became locked to me
When we grew apart
Just when I thought I'd escaped the dusty gray
I find myself breathing yesterday

I've decided I don't want to say goodbye to you anymore
The consequences are far more than I can take
I once let you go, but I'm gonna reopen that door
'Cause letting go a second time may be my biggest mistake

I've found myself
Discontent in breathing yesterday
There's a ringing in my memory
I tried to hide away
And I'm diving down
To the depths of my heart
That became locked to me
When we grew apart
Just when I thought I'd escaped the dusty gray
I find myself breathing yesterday

Upon finishing the song, Meghan returned to the beginning and read it again. She was confident a wealth of details remained hidden, and she would need to search beneath the surface to bring them forth.

Her estimation proved correct.

Halfway through her third reading, her hand dropped. Eyes wide open, Meghan lay against the ground, staring at the sapphire sky as it darkened. Her heart felt as though its flesh had been rubbed sore. A tear seared her cheek as it straggled down her face and settled in her ear.

Wiping her eyes, she gripped the letter with both hands, her will caught in a tug-of-war. No matter how sudden the song's arrival, and regardless of what had prompted Danny to send it at this point in time, Meghan knew she couldn't ignore it if she tried.

She faced a decision, and it was strategic.
She felt so ill-equipped.

CHAPTER 21
AUGUST 2007

Danny lit a cigarette and walked along the footbridge at The Landing. On this late August afternoon, most schools were now in session around the country, and Sunset Beach, in keeping with its annual cycle, had returned to a state of eerie desolation. In a few weeks, the temperature would begin a noticeable decline.

Two months had passed since Danny had sent "Breathing Yesterday" to Meghan Harting.

Two months without a reply.

No doubt, she had received his letter. After all, it had not been returned to sender. He'd expected a delayed response, but after two months with no indication of Meghan's feelings, Danny had concluded Meghan needed something else, more than Danny could provide. Something beyond a timing. Something unidentified, yet clearly absent.

Maybe Meghan loved Brian after all.

Shaking his head in disbelief, Danny felt a bit gullible and wondered how he'd managed to convince himself that Meghan would return to him. When he'd sent the letter initially, he had sculpted several reunion scenarios in his mind. But after the first month passed, his hopes had started to wane.

On numerous occasions, fantasies had sparked within him as he constructed possible reactions on Meghan's part, the many what-if factors. But in the end, in this moment, Danny acknowledged all the what-ifs and maybes carried no bearing whatsoever. In their place stood a solitary absolute: Reality, in all its harsh glory, will trump guesswork every time.

Oddly enough, Danny found himself content with the outcome, gritty as it was. Through a personal discovery process, he had developed his own view of destiny, an amalgamation of input he had received from different sources. Yielding to Reece's advice, Danny had birthed a new song, one in which he had given his heart apt representation. Danny had also judged Jay's perception of destiny accurate, a series of choices and action.

Danny still believed he and Meghan were designed for each other. Nevertheless, he had also come to the conclusion that, while a person might possess a sense of fate within, such a notion was insufficient on its own. Rather, when destiny involved two people, it arrived with two sets of choices. It required each individual to listen to his or her heart, then choose to follow his or her own inclinations. Unfortunately, if either individual denied his or her heart's cry, destiny would lose.

Destiny lost a battle at Sunset Beach, South Carolina.

Danny drew in another cloud of smoke and released it through his lips in a tight stream of tobacco apparition. How could someone fail to recognize, or perhaps ignore, a desire of the heart, a rhythmic bellow that relented with each beat until heeded? At least, that was how he perceived it. Meghan had made her decision. He couldn't understand her choice but knew he must accept it unconditionally, the same manner in which he loved her.

Danny groaned. Meghan would always occupy a piece of his heart, and he knew it well.

For Danny, "Breathing Yesterday" marked the end of an era and the beginning of a new phase in his life. To his dismay, this upcoming phase would not include the girl he loved. Nonetheless, the era was indeed fresh. While it would commence with emptiness, Danny also found a kind of peace inherent in it, a tranquility in knowing he had taken every available step to avoid it.

Leaning over the ledge, Danny kicked a pebble into the lake and watched the ripples of water circle outward in liquid telepathy. He had come to Sunset Beach to escape the memories of Meghan that hung frozen in the crisp Ohio cold. He had opted instead for the pleasant distraction of waves, sand and sun index. But now the time had come for his next course of action, which Danny determined would be a departure. After all, he couldn't spend the remainder of his life here in aimless solitude.

As usual, Danny knew not what the future held for him. However, he figured the most appropriate plan would be to return home and face his new, ordinary lifestyle with boldness. Besides, even if Meghan changed her mind, he had provided his cell phone number in the letter, so she could reach him if she wanted to. But he wouldn't raise his hopes.

A plan of attack ran through his mind. Danny would submit two weeks' notice to Jay in the morning. He would browse the Internet and reserve a rental truck, which he knew Jay would be willing to help load. Once he reached Ohio, Danny would rent a storage compartment for his furniture while he searched for employment. Since his funds were limited, he would wait until he secured a job before looking for an apartment. His parents would allow him to live at home on a temporary basis until that occurred. They would be thrilled to hear he'd come to his senses and wanted to leave the beach behind.

Soon, Danny would occupy a cubicle in the silent corridor of a mortgage company or bank office and return to his old professional stride. Instead of the waves of the Atlantic, maybe he could settle for the subtle motion of Lake Erie.

Danny's heart sank.

Eyes shut, he took a deep breath. He was confident that, at any given moment, no matter where he lived, he would pick up the faint scent of the salty ocean air. Without a doubt, he would miss the minor details of his almost-paradise.

One final inhale of smoke. Danny gazed with longing at the water and flicked the cigarette butt into the open air before him, much like he had released his dream to a destiny unfulfilled. A light breeze carried the cigarette a few extra feet before it landed on the water's surface. The cigarette's orange sparks trailed close behind, then diminished. Danny related to the orange sparks.

Danny Bale picked at a splinter on the ledge, then headed toward the parking lot.

CHAPTER 22
SEPTEMBER 30, 2000

Book bag over his shoulder, Danny walked through the dorm building's main entrance. He'd stopped by the library to do some quick research after class, and now, at 4:40 p.m., his stomach growled for dinner.

Walking past the information desk, he bent over and looked through the tiny, plastic window on his mailbox, which revealed a single envelope inside. Thrilled with what he saw, Danny forgot to shut the mailbox door.

A letter from Meghan.

Danny didn't want to waste time racing up the stairs. Instead, he jogged toward the lounge, where a group of students sat engrossed in a soap opera on the big-screen television. From within earshot of the program, he caught a smattering of the dialogue and deduced the clichéd story line: a man on trial for murder, a woman in love with his brother, and a hooker with evidence that could turn the verdict's tide—but not until November sweeps, Danny guessed.

Danny wondered how Meghan had reacted to his letter. He had just sent it the previous week. Surely her quick response was a good sign. He glanced at the envelope's lower corner, where he noticed she had sketched a happy face. Detail by detail, his prospects seemed to improve.

Settling into a bulky, beverage-stained chair in one corner of the room, Danny plopped his book bag on the floor and opened the letter. Ever since sending "Meghan's Song" to her, Danny had made a daily ritual of checking his mailbox first thing after class. His excitement had surged each time he saw mail in the box, followed by disappointment at an absence of correspondence from Meghan. Although Danny knew his wait could have lasted much longer, the days had still felt like weeks.

He admired Meghan's flowing script as he took his time reading her letter:

Danny,

Hi! How's the Atlantic coast? Okay, it's not exactly the coast, but you're a whole lot closer to it than I'd ever expect to end up!

First of all, let me say that "Meghan's Song" is absolutely beautiful—at least, the words are beautiful, and I'm sure the music follows suit. I wish I played an instrument so I could hear it! Your song—and the simple fact that you thought of me that way—touched my heart more than you can imagine. Clearly, it came from deep inside. Thank you for treating me the way you do. I think you see me better than I see myself.

Secondly, you need to know that your friendship means so much to me. You're one of the few people who have stood by my side regardless of the circumstances, and I don't think you'll ever be aware of how you lifted my head when my world came crashing down. I've never forgotten it and never will.

The next part of this letter is the hardest for me to write. I have to admit, your letter caught me by surprise and forced me to evaluate life, where I've been and where I'm going, and it's been a difficult decision to make. I do remember the time you referred to when I was pregnant and we talked on my couch. The month or two before it had been very tough, and talking openly with you was like much-needed therapy for me. I remember how you listened and stared into my eyes, and I've sensed a strong connection with you ever since then. Danny, you will always have a place in my heart that no one else could ever fill. You have a bright future ahead of you.

No matter how I put it, these words are going to sound coldhearted, so you need to know it has nothing to do with you as a person.

At that point, Meghan must have paused to ponder her remarks. Danny noticed a subtle change in the pressure of her penmanship, an attribute that would have escaped him had he not scrutinized each word on the page. When Meghan resumed, she had pressed her pen harder against the paper, perhaps with intensified concentration.

But to be honest, I don't think a long-distance relationship would be good for either of us. At this point in my life, I feel like I need to stay with Brian. All I can say is—for reasons not even I can grasp—I need to make this work with him. Somehow I hope you'll understand. I know he loves me, so you won't need to worry about my settling for second best.

Just now, I stopped and read what I've written so far.

Danny, I don't want you to be hurt. You're such a great guy, and let's face it, you would be making a mistake by getting involved with me anyway. I could end up hurting you just like I've managed to hurt myself with all the mistakes I've made. I mean, I'm already hurting you with this letter. After a while, you'll see that this is best. Trust me, the right girl is out there, and she's going to be wonderful—because *you're* wonderful.

I hope we can stay friends, but if you never want to talk to me again, I understand. I'm so sorry.

A piece of my heart will always belong to you, Danny.

Meghan

After a prolonged stare at the page, Danny refolded the letter. This was not the response he'd expected. In fact, with each passing day, he had managed to chip away at the possibility of her rejection. After all, he had exposed his soul in his letter to her.

Numb, Danny shook his head, unable to comprehend Meghan's reply.

How could someone know they are so loved, yet offer a simple "I'm sorry" in response? Surely she had overlooked a detail in his letter. Or maybe some of the memories they shared had slipped her mind.

Yet in his heart, Danny knew such prospects were imaginary. He knew Meghan had taken care to prepare an accurate reply.

CHAPTER 23
SEPTEMBER 2007

Where would she have put those old videos? thought Brian as he stood in the bedroom doorway, hands rested on his hips. Earlier on the phone, Meghan had made evening plans for the two of them to get together with a group of friends, a conversation culminating with her promise to bring along a 1980s Brat Pack film. They had stashed their videocassette collection somewhere in the house but had forgotten its location. Before Meghan had left a few minutes ago, Brian had offered to find the movie. He had already scoured the basement and den without success.

As he scanned their bedroom, he looked toward the bed, then remembered they had shoved nothing underneath it but an old set of dumbbells Meghan had owned before they lived together.

Confident the videos weren't lurking in his own closet, he opened Meghan's, where a row of clothes on hangers greeted him. Shoeboxes lined the floor, and a column of narrow shelves, mounted to one side of the closet, contained a bouquet of seldom-worn sweaters and casual items. Peering up, Brian surveyed a shelf that hung atop the hanger rack, a few inches over his head. It was lined with purses, of which he recognized three and doubted Meghan would ever use the others.

Another glance at the purses and he noticed they sat toward the shelf's front edge, probably guarding another row of items behind them. To get a look at what sat toward the back of the shelf, he hopped on one foot but glimpsed nothing more than a dust bunny suspended behind pair of purse handles. Leaping higher, he finally saw small stacks of videocassettes behind the purses, their jackets faded from exposure to light and the course of time. For a moment, he considered grabbing a chair from the kitchen to reach them but, in optimistic male judgment, he decided the effort to retrieve a single movie was not worth the trip.

Jiggling the side shelves and finding them steady, Brian stepped with caution onto the bottom shelf and grabbed hold of the purse shelf, securing himself at a near forty-five degree angle. He discovered the film—at the other end of the shelf, albeit on the top of its stack.

With a single-handed grip on the upper shelf, Brian reached out and swatted at the videocassette with his free hand. Unsuccessful at first, he stretched a bit farther and lost his balance in the process. He swiped the film's corner in a final attempt, sending the video in a free fall to the ground, Brian himself not far behind. The closet door banged into the wall as his body crashed against it. By accident, on his way down, he swept his foot over the array of shoeboxes and scattered boxes and lids across the floor.

Brian rolled his eyes. A single movie was not worth this punishment.

Brian flung the video onto the bed and started matching shoeboxes with lids, trying to recall their original arrangement—an honorable endeavor, but also short-lived. He decided to simply stack boxes as seemed reasonable, trying to keep the similar sets together. And to his amateur eyes, there were many similar pairs. Brian chuckled as he recalled the limited selection of shoes in his own closet. And each of his shoes survived without a box, left exposed to the harsh interior air.

Reaching for the next box to match with a lid, he stopped short when he noticed a yellow shoebox, the lid of which had wobbled out of place and revealed a peculiarity: the shoebox contained no shoes. Instead, he saw a small, white envelope peeking out of the box, jostled out of place during the disturbance.

Although he chose to ignore it at first, the envelope continued to tease his curiosity until he pulled it out of the box, peering over his shoulder as though Meghan were in the next room. When he flipped the white piece over, he discovered it had originated from Danny Bale at the University of North Carolina several years ago. It resembled the letter Brian had found stuffed in the bookshelf a few months ago, the one Meghan had shrugged off and torn into pieces.

Shocked, Brian bit his lip and removed the shoebox lid to expose a box filled with envelopes like the one he held in his hand. Sifting through half of them, he discovered Danny Bale had sent each one. Eyes blade-sharp with suspicion, carefully Brian packed the letters back into the shoebox and replaced its lid, sliding the box back to where Meghan had, as far as he could tell, hidden it.

Brian continued to set the remaining shoeboxes in order.

• • •

"I don't want to spend an hour in the grocery store," Meghan announced from the passenger seat the next day. "So whatever you need, go get it when we walk in the door, okay?"

Brian turned a corner, then relaxed his hand and allowed the steering wheel to glide back to center position. "Booze and smokes it is," he joshed.

"Funny. Don't blame me for wasting money, then."

Meghan stuck her hand out the window and savored the rush of cool, hazy breeze against her palm. She allowed the air to lift her hand in a manner akin to an airplane's ascent. At last, after two rocky months, she could concentrate on something other than Danny's "Breathing Yesterday" letter. Over the past few weeks, as she'd become engrossed in her daily routine, the emotional tug of his recent correspondence crept further toward her subconscious. Although the topic lingered in the back of her mind, the normality of this present moment provided a pleasant distraction. For the first time since the arrival of "Breathing Yesterday," Meghan could ignore the conflict that had churned within her.

Almost.

If Danny were in the vehicle right now, Meghan thought, she would probably tell him to get rid of a cigarette, feigning disgust but secretly glad he sat beside her at the wheel. He would respond with a clever remark, and she would duck back as he reached across to flick the ashes out her window for laughs. At that point, she would push aside his arm, the one with the tiny scar. As kids, Danny had tried to impress her with an attempt to jump the fence that surrounded his neighbor's yard—a feat that had ended in minor tragedy. An inch short of clearance, he had scraped his arm across the upper edge of the fence's aluminum links. Eight-year-old Danny's tears had escalated at the sight of a lone trickle of blood. Ten years later, the same Danny would boast of the battle wound he'd suffered on her behalf, insisting that scars are sexy.

Meghan couldn't help but grin.

Sexy. Right.

Interrupting her memory drift, Brian glanced in her direction, then back at the road, then at Meghan again, but tried to appear casual.

"So, uh, about this Danny guy your family knows—what exactly went on between you two?"

Brian's question caught her by surprise. Meghan punted with a nonchalant veneer of her own. "Not much. We were good friends at one point, but then the years went by and so did our lives. We lost touch." Suspended somewhere between guilt and longing, Meghan still couldn't decide how to react to Danny's renewed chivalry in the form of his letter. It wasn't her fault he had composed a new song for her. After all, she hadn't prompted his gesture. But the fact that she had welcomed it made her feel as though she had been unfaithful to Brian, even though she hadn't.

"Does he know we're still together?" Brian asked.

"I'd imagine he does."

"Does he know we've been living together?"

"Are you jealous?"

"Just curious, that's all. Don't you ever get curious enough to touch bases with him? I mean, you two wrote back and forth for quite a while, right?"

In a huff, Meghan said, "I can't believe you're this upset over finding one letter I'd stuck inside a book years ago and forgotten about. I tore it up in front of your eyes, remember?"

"Oh, don't give me that! I found them, Meghan—*all* of them."

"Stuck in another book, I suppose?"

"They're tucked away in your closet, inside a yellow shoebox, mixed together with the other boxes."

Speechless, Meghan squinted at him. Though she hid the fact that she was stunned, anger rippled inside her. She pursed her lips as she looked out the window.

Brian prodded further. "Shoebox sound familiar?"

Meghan glared straight at him. "What were you doing in my closet?"

"I was looking for that movie you asked me to find. When I stood on a shelf to reach it, I slipped and knocked the boxes over. An envelope was sticking out of the box, so I looked to see what else was in the box, and the letters were all there—right where you left them."

"So you went ahead and sifted through the whole box?"

"Wouldn't you think it was strange if you found a stack of letters in *my* closet from an old girlfriend?"

"He's not an old boyfriend, Brian. And regardless of how odd it might seem, I wouldn't invade your privacy like that!"

She could see Brian glare at her through his sunglasses.

"Are you still into this guy?" he asked.

Irritable, Meghan underscored each syllable with firm enunciation. "No, Brian."

"Well, you must keep his letters around for *some* reason," he sneered.

"It's not like you ever bother to do anything like that. Danny has a romantic side to him, and I can appreciate that."

"You can't let go, and neither can he!" Brian chortled, his head cocked. "He actually had the nerve to write to you from some beach."

"What?" Confused, Meghan quickly recounted the days

since Danny's "Breathing Yesterday" letter had arrived. She hadn't taken it into the house, and she was the one who had found it sitting in the mailbox. How could Brian have known about it? "When did *you* see his letter from the beach?"

"He sent it a few years ago."

"A few years ago? I don't know what you're talking about."

"That's because I threw it in the trash before you got home."

A different letter?

Meghan seethed. "I suppose you read that letter too?"

"Absolutely! Wouldn't you?"

"You're pathetic! Where do you get the idea that you control me? Do you think I'm so needy that I'm going to put up with this forever?"

"As if you had other options! Who's gonna knock on the door of a girl who's already been knocked up once before?"

Meghan bit her lip. Her chest felt cut. "Let me tell you something about Danny: He loves me regardless of what happened in the past. And *I'm* comfortable regardless of the past. At least he encourages me for who I am—and he doesn't shred me apart in the process!"

"Go ahead and side with him, Meghan." Brian's jaw grew rigid. "Tough life that guy has—soaking in the sun, strumming a guitar all day. Wait a minute, he does have a job. What does he do? Flip burgers? Pitiful."

"He puts as much sweat equity into his 'pitiful' job as you put into yours. And at least he's got a passion inside of him. He pays a price to be able to speak to people's hearts, and that's not something you can buy with money. For that matter, neither am I!"

Brian laughed.

Meghan felt her eyes sharpen. "All right, stop the car," she ordered.

"What? Why?"

"I'm getting out. I don't want to argue about this anymore."

"So, you just want me to drop you on the side of the street? How will you get home?"

"I'll grab a cab. I don't care."

Rolling his eyes, Brian said, "Meghan, cool down. I wasn't serious anyway."

"Stop the car, Brian."

"Aren't you overreacting?"

Meghan unbuckled her seat belt. "Stop the car right now."

His face now red with fury, Brian swerved to the side of the road and slammed on the brakes. Before the car reached a full stop, Meghan had already opened the door. Climbing out, she slammed it shut and stormed in the opposite direction. Brian pounded his fist against the dashboard.

With her back to the silver BMW, Meghan heard its wheels screech away.

Her feet pounded against the concrete sidewalk, each step releasing a notch of tension like wading through waist-deep sand. Her mind felt cluttered beyond capacity, and she couldn't pause to think. Her patience had grown restless to the point of severity. A change was imminent, Meghan was well aware.

She marched past random passersby, searched for a taxi company on her cell phone, and called a cab. Deep down, she had wanted to call it for years but had yielded to fear—fear of the unknown, fear of reality.

Meghan's stomach went numb. In the course of fearing failure, she had failed to listen to her heart.

Meghan regretted losing Danny.

She always had.

CHAPTER 24
SEPTEMBER 2007

One week later, Meghan left the house a few minutes past 10 a.m. in an effort to avoid facing Brian, who always slept late on Saturday mornings. Her sole plan for the day was to keep her distance from him—or maybe the other way around. After pulling her car into a rear parking lot in uptown Oxford, she walked along a side street and turned the corner at a double-screen cinema that possessed a semi-historic tone, its concrete exterior painted and repainted through the years.

She paraded past a series of parking meters and mom-and-pop store windows, down a sidewalk populated by local families and college students who had returned for the fall semester. As she examined the local spouses and their broods of kids, Meghan pictured herself one day holding hands with a child of her own and guiding him—or her—across the street. When crossing the street, though, she wouldn't allow her kids to dodge vehicles, as she did at the moment. Like a good mom, she would lead them across the street within the safe borders of a crosswalk.

Meghan arrived at a bar and grill, the windows of which had clouded with age, its wooden door in dire need of a dark brown stain. Inside, she made her way toward the bar counter, where she spotted an open stool beside a thirty-something stranger, the back of whose head she could have sworn was Danny Bale's before she caught a glimpse of the man's face. Her sentiment kicking into gear, Meghan sat beside the stranger but paid no further attention to him.

When the bartender stopped by, she ordered a grilled chicken sandwich and iced tea, then swung around to face the other side of the room, where a small, makeshift platform fit surprisingly well within the narrow confines of the establishment's brick walls. The platform, a structure built with spare plywood and the ingenuity of employees with extra time to kill, was draped with maroon fabric and crowned with a mismatched chair. On the platform, a female performer, a clear amateur, picked at a guitar and made a feeble attempt to sing an original tune. In Meghan's estimation, the girl appeared to be out of her element before an audience.

Meghan's mind drifted to Danny. Later that night, on the South Carolina coast, he would sing onstage like this singer, Meghan figured. She imagined what it must be like to watch him perform for a crowd, strumming his guitar at a place called McGrady's, but with greater deftness than the singer in this room.

What's Danny doing right now, right at this moment? Meghan wondered. She considered the possibilities: Watching the waves frolic, perhaps? Taking a walk along a stretch of warm, gray sand? Or working in a hot kitchen, preparing a chicken sandwich like the one Meghan had just ordered?

She admired Danny's courage to follow his heart's desire. In retrospect, she wished he had asked her to join him there, but acknowledged that window of opportunity had closed when she'd chosen a relationship with Brian.

The stranger who sat beside Meghan swirled around on his stool and nodded toward the singer. "That's gotta be harder than it looks. You wouldn't see me up there."

Meghan wasn't interested in talking, but his remark spurred a reaction in her. "Yeah, but they love performing for people. I have a friend who does the same thing."

"Here in town?"

"South Carolina. A bar and grill at Sunset Beach."

The singer now grasped at a high note. A noble effort—and a bungled one. Meghan cringed on the inside but tried to maintain a straight face. She sympathized with the artist, who seemed oblivious to the fact that her high pitch resembled the cry of a wounded squirrel.

"I hope your friend's material is better than that!" the stranger said, then spun back around. Apparently he found more entertainment in his mug of beer.

Indeed, Danny could run circles around this performer. Then again, this performer didn't have much to run with, period.

"Yeah, my friend's amazing," Meghan replied, now wondering if Danny had ever sung "Meghan's Song" or "Breathing Yesterday" on a weekend night. Maybe she should write and ask him to record one of his performances so she could listen to his song set.

"You teach at the university?" Meghan's barstool neighbor asked.

She offered no response. In a peculiar way, she had become absorbed in the performance at hand and allowed the stranger's question to fade in her mind.

Her heart racing, Meghan grew hot and felt beads of perspiration surface at the roots of her hair. She ran her fingers through her wavy locks. When she reached for her iced tea, the liquid sloshed in the glass. Meghan noticed her hand shook mildly, which she chalked up to a low sugar level at first.

As she grew more anxious, her stomach began to sour, and she realized her physical state had nothing to do with nutrition.

Meghan slammed her the glass on the counter. She rustled through her purse, pulled out a crisp twenty, and motioned for the bartender's attention. "Excuse me!"

The bartender approached and, upon spotting Meghan's half-full glass, asked if he could get her a refill. Then he mentioned her face had become a shade paler and asked if she felt okay. The stranger beside Meghan cocked his head in Meghan's direction while he examined his beer mug as if to strategize where he would place his lips for the next gulp.

Meghan felt her whole face grow hot.

"I'm sorry, but I won't be able to stay and eat," she said, hopping down from the stool and slapping her cash on the counter. "This should cover the bill and a tip. Thanks anyway."

A perplexed expression on his face, the bartender watched as Meghan zipped her purse and rushed for the front door. On her way out, she brushed past an incoming customer and left an apology in her wake.

• • •

In the bedroom, Meghan opened a bulky, blue-and-green duffel bag on the bed. Her anxiety advanced to desperation as she darted around the room, grabbing a couple of shirts from the closet and folding them in haste. Her hands continued to quiver.

Brian wasn't home, but her boyfriend wasn't foremost on

her mind.

After stuffing the shirts into her duffel bag, she made her way to the dresser and treated a few pairs of socks in the same manner, followed by shorts and other articles of clothing in no particular order. Casual was her goal, her method spontaneous. She ran to the bathroom and grabbed a handful of necessities—hairbrush, toothbrush, makeup.

Zipping the bag, she took a final glance around the room to make sure she hadn't forgotten any essentials. A heavy packer by her own admission, Meghan packed uncharacteristically light this time.

She didn't care. She had to get out the door.

Purse and keys in hand, duffel bag strapped upon her shoulder, she looked at her watch, which read 11:13 a.m. She would need to travel fast in a race against sunset.

In her hurry, Meghan almost forgot to lock the door to the house on her way out. She threw her bag and purse on the passenger seat of her car.

Meghan dashed out of the neighborhood in her Honda. A handful of rural streets and a couple of highways later, she would merge onto Interstate 75, where she would surpass the speed limit by a hefty margin.

CHAPTER 25
SEPTEMBER 2007

"Thank you," Danny spoke into the microphone, acknowledging the applause and whistles that followed his sturdy performance. He would miss his weekends on the McGrady's stage, Saturday nights like tonight, particularly the subtleties so easy to take for granted: the applause, the smoky ambience, and his inexplicable connection with the audience.

From ten feet away in the audience, a redhead winked at him, to which he nodded with appreciation. He pointed his next comment in her direction, as if he'd molded his words for her ears exclusively. "I'm Danny Bale. Gonna take a little break and be back in a few. I'd buy ya'll a round of drinks, but they pay me in nickels around here." The redhead smiled wider before her boyfriend nudged her.

Resting his guitar against the back wall of the platform, Danny descended the steps and made his way toward the rear exit, where Jay stood in a florescent T-shirt. Arms crossed, Jay resembled a bouncer more than a manager. Slapping Danny on the back as he approached, he wore a toothy grin.

"Your last night, Danny Boy," Jay said. "I guess it'll be me and a karaoke machine next week."

Danny shook his head and snickered, relishing the thought of Jay's shaggy hair swaying to a Paul Simon song. Actually, make that Carly Simon. Danny chuckled louder.

Jay's humorous eyes narrowed. "You're imagining me on that stage, aren't you?"

"Yep." Circa 1972, with his head wrapped in a Rhoda Morgenstern-looking scarf.

"James Taylor?"

"Paul Simon." Jay would kill him if he knew about the scarf image.

"When do you want me to stop by and help you load the truck for the big move?" Jay asked.

"Next Saturday morning, if that's okay. I'll spend the week packing. Maybe catch a few extra rays before leaving."

Jay examined his alleged protégé and nodded. Danny could see admiration in Jay's eyes. "I'm proud of ya, guy. I guess your destiny changes course tonight, huh?"

Danny shrugged. No more rounds of drinks after work. No more blind dates courtesy of Jay. Just a steady job and a steady savings account to match. Danny grinned at the thought of a 401(k).

Finding themselves in uncharted territory tonight, each friend formed a fist and bumped knuckles with the other.

Jay jerked his thumb over his shoulder and winked. "Hurry up with that break. Don't keep my customers waiting."

Pausing for a moment, the reality of good-bye settled into Danny's gut. He feigned a lopsided salute to his chief and wandered out the back door.

Outside, Danny breathed in the humid, yet chilly, air, which soothed him as he gazed at the sky. Daylight's final minutes. The eastern horizon was a dark, star-embedded canvas, its western counterpart a fainting blue fire.

For one last time, Danny decided to spend his break at the footbridge, his regular routine. As he meandered toward it, he scoped out The Landing's Saturday night window shoppers. Pleased that the tourists had returned to their nests until next year, the locals who tended to avoid the site during the summer months now constituted The Landing's core patronage. The population had diminished considerably, along with the number of shopping bags in hand. Most passersby were here to soak in the atmosphere and enjoy the community they called home.

Walking to the distant end of the footbridge, a bit farther than usual, Danny stopped at a random spot, where he leaned over the ledge, rapt with the moonlight that shimmered on the ripples of water. The lake seemed to lose some of its magic when September arrived, but this natural luminescence seemed to inject it with fresh life.

For Danny, life would be unfamiliar without the prospect of Meghan returning to him. While the outcome was not what he had hoped, in the fiber of his heart he was confident he had come close. He had missed by just a few years and a few hundred miles. But he would never know for sure. Mysteries are notorious for unanswered questions that deaden the heart.

He peered across the lake to the other side, where a collection of people wrapped up their activities before The Landing closed for the night. A concluding carousel spin. A final snow cone. One last trip to the photo booth for a cheeky pose.

Danny angled his watch toward the light of a lamppost. Time to head back to the restaurant and bring closure to an era on stage.

Pushing away from the ledge, he ran tired fingers through

his hair, which would soon return to its darker shade of blond in the Ohio cold. He started his walk across the bridge, where sunset's swan song barely made the random faces of oncoming pedestrians distinguishable.

Suddenly, from halfway across the bridge, his eyes locked with those of a familiar face. Perplexed, Danny Bale squinted, leaning his head forward with caution. His bones felt fluidic as curiosity lured him forward.

She must have come from McGrady's and now made her way toward him from the end of the bridge. Slowly, Danny inched in the direction of the girl, who smiled, tears running from her eyes and glimmering in the moonlight. Danny opened his eyes wide and mouthed his response in a tone barely audible to his own ears.

"Meghan ..."

Overshadowed by instinct, Danny began to jog toward her, dodging people along the way without breaking his focus. Meghan drew closer to him, her pace on the rise, her tears more evident to Danny with each step she took. Danny would have mistaken her image as a mirage, were his heart not aching with the same bittersweet tinge he had felt for her at age fifteen.

They convened beneath a lamppost and stood face to face, motionless. To Danny, Meghan's visage appeared a bit older than when he had last seen her. Nonetheless, as he gazed into the depths of her blue eyes, their familiarity struck him in an instant. Danny saw the girl with whom he had fallen in love a lifetime ago.

Without a word, he placed his hand on her face and smoothed away the tears from her cheeks.

Meghan seemed overcome with relief and sniffled as she waved a large envelope, folded in half. As her hand dropped back to her side, Danny recognized the item as the letter containing his final song for her.

She had come.

He blinked, yet she remained before him.

Destiny Landing, indeed.

By accident, a single laugh of joy escaped Danny's mouth. He felt breathless.

Reaching out, he drew her close and wrapped her in his arms like a fragile angel. A perfect fit within his embrace. He had missed that most of all.

As a tear straggled down his face, he placed his hand upon the small of her back with delicate care. And once again, she met him halfway.

Gently, for the first time in his life, Danny pressed his lips against hers.

EPILOGUE
CHRISTMAS EVE 1979

Wrapped in red paper speckled with mistletoe print and topped with a shiny white bow, the slender box was only twelve inches long, yet it seemed to double in size when Meghan held it against her tiny body. Meghan's curiosity loomed larger.

She knew she shouldn't. Even at three, she was well aware the gift wasn't intended for her pudgy, preschool hands. But it looked so pretty.

Meghan scooted a smidgen to the right, her back toward the adults in the room. Compared to the size of the other gifts, this box looked like it might have come from her dollhouse back home. What could possibly hide inside such a cute treasure?

No, she shouldn't do it.

Well, maybe just a quick look.

A grin, impish yet innocent, cracked across her face as she peeked over her shoulder to see if anyone was watching. She couldn't wait any longer.

Running her finger along the back of the gift where the paper's two edges met, she ripped around the tape. Off came the paper to expose a bare, white box. Meghan thought the box would look prettier with balloons on it.

Lifting the lid, she discovered a navy blue necktie, folded upon a cotton cushion.

Jumping to her feet, Meghan thrust her hands on her waist in the candid manner of a three-year-old and remarked, "I don't want a tie!" She made a goofy facial expression … and then remembered what she had left behind a minute earlier.

Spinning around, she saw little Danny, still on the floor, enthralled with his new sponge toy. Meghan hopped over to the boy, sugar from an eggnog overload running rampant through her veins.

"I'm back, Danny!" she said and plopped down next to him, wrapping her arm around him once again. He smelled fresh, a cross between nursery-sterile and baby-bath clean. Danny blurbed something in a language of his own, which Meghan thought adorable. Squeezing the fourteen-month-old with a delicate side hug, she took no offense that Danny was oblivious of her affection.

With tender care, the manner her parents had deemed proper for a baby, Meghan kissed the blond boy on the head.

"I love you, baby Danny."

Also Available

John Herrick's novel

FROM THE DEAD

Turn the page for a preview >>

About *From the Dead*

A preacher's son. A father in hiding. A guilty heart filled with secrets.

When Jesse Barlow escaped to Hollywood at age eighteen, he hungered for freedom, fame and fortune. Eleven years later, his track record of failure results in a drug-induced suicide attempt. Revived at death's doorstep, Jesse returns to his Ohio hometown to make amends with his preacher father, a former lover, and Jesse's own secret son. But Jesse's renewed commitment becomes a baptism by fire when his son's advanced illness calls for a sacrifice—one that could cost Jesse the very life he regained. A story of mercy, hope, and second chances, From the Dead captures the human spirit with tragedy and joy.

CHAPTER 1

J ADA Ferrari lit the collection of miniature candles along the coffee table. Darkness evaporated from the living room.

As Jada leaned forward, Jesse Barlow admired the curvature of her figure, the way her brunette hair fell in curls past her shoulder blades.

"I just bought these today," said Jada, who brushed her hand above the flames and sent the aroma of jasmine wafting through the air. Ever the center of attention, she sat on the edge of the sofa beside Cameron and Gavin, friends from an apartment downstairs, as Gavin lit the round of joints.

The scene, once common, had grown less frequent in recent months. Nowadays, Jada, a burgeoning film director's assistant, sought company with people who could further her career.

Jesse's career, on the other hand, begged resuscitation.

From the recliner at the far end of the room, Jesse, distant and disengaged, stared out the window at the crisp glow of a streetlight two stories below. At the chirp of an activated car alarm, Jesse leaned toward the sound in time to see a male silhouette emerge from the shadows and wander into the apartment building next door.

An anonymous man. Los Angeles is filled with them.

Then again, everyone is anonymous to someone. And everyone has an anonymous side, a shadow within, a guarded corner where secrets hide.

Gavin passed a joint to Jada. With a puff, she held her breath, coughed a few times, then fell back against the cushions and hung limber, as though she'd craved this all day.

Cameron grinned. "Next time, you buy."

Spoken like a low-level accountant.

Jada waved her joint toward Jesse in a hypnotic-like motion. "Are you gonna keep staring out the window or get in on the act?"

Years ago, he wouldn't have hesitated. Never an addict or heavy user, Jesse enjoyed a recreational hit when the urge mounted within. But the pleasure had long passed. He'd grown tired of breathing the strange air, the subtle loss of control.

He wished his guests would leave but knew it would be a few hours. Soon the music would start—Beck's Odelay, no doubt—followed by a raid on his refrigerator. Gavin and Cameron would argue whether "Loser" or "Where It's At" was the singer's breakthrough single.

Oh, what the hell. "All right, hand one over." And with that, Jesse reached out his thumb and forefinger.

"There you go." Jada beamed as she passed Jesse a joint. "You never have fun anymore. Gotta live a little!" She turned to her couch mates. "Right, losers?"

Lightheaded, Gavin giggled.

With the joint in his fingers, Jesse sank into the recliner once again. He yielded to the sharp herbal fumes that crept like a current through his veins and loosened his brain. The effect seemed immediate, his body no longer conditioned to the stuff. He focused on the array of candles as their flames increased in clarity and the jasmine grew richer.

Gavin exhaled a deep cloud and leered at oblivion, a pensive look on his face like a stoned Socrates. He waved his joint in front of his face, as if in afterthought. "You know, those Rasta-fari guys say this stuff helps you get close to God."

God, thought Jesse. The God who never seemed to give him answers to a lifetime of questions. And as Jesse sat, present yet isolated, those questions resurfaced in a torrent.

Why did she have to die?

Why did I leave them behind?

Jesse leaned back further against the black leather cushion and clenched his jaw.

I'm a preacher's son, he thought.

So how did my life get so fucked up?

CHAPTER 2

THE screech of an alarm clock pierced the 3:30 a.m. silence. Jada, groggy from the night before, groaned as she felt around the pre-dawn darkness for the button to make the ringing stop. Not one to snooze, she sat up in a heap as Jesse rolled over and mumbled.

"Is Barry scheduling sunrise meetings now?" Jesse asked.

Barry Richert. The Barry Richert, as Jada reminded everyone who would listen. Barry Richert, whose unexpected success arrived two years ago with a low-budget film that became a sleeper hit. These days, the man received hundreds of screenplays a week.

"A location shoot in Malibu. Call time is seven, but he needs me there an hour early."

Her commute from their Sherman Oaks apartment would require less than an hour, but Jesse knew Jada would spend much longer perfecting her image in the bathroom. She pressed her fingers against her head, which must have continued to pulsate from the prior evening's get-together.

"Go back to sleep, babe." She stroked his chest once and climbed out of bed. Jesse leaned on an elbow and eyed the silhouette of his girlfriend, clad in a slinky black negligee, as she tiptoed across the crowded bedroom and turned on the bathroom light.

Through the cracked door, Jesse heard the sputter of a shower. Then he buried his head in the pillow and dozed off. He had come to dread the sunrise in recent months.

* * *

"A polarizing filter will help reduce glare," Jesse explained. "Kind of like wearing a pair of shades at the beach." From a display rack on the sales floor, he peered out the window while, for the sixth time, he rattled off the benefits of camera filters to a newbie.

"What about this one?" asked the customer, who grabbed a transparent red filter from the rack and held it toward the overhead light. "It looks like half a pair of 3-D glasses."

"More or less. It can be used to cover up skin blemishes. Heavy acne, that sort of thing," Jesse said.

The customer chuckled in a series of mother-hen clucks. She tucked a lock of silvering chestnut hair behind her ear and said, "That would come in handy for my daughter-in-law. The latest one, that is. Spent thousands on a boob job but can't get rid of that acne along her neckline. Spends half her life in the tanning booth to cover it up. That reminds me: Can any of these filter things hide my son's inheritance from her?"

"Sorry, ma'am."

LensPerfection sat on Ventura Boulevard near the Van Nuys intersection. Crammed within a dense stretch of bricked retail, the photography shop shared its walls with a Java Cup coffee shop on one side and an incense store on the other. Jesse found humor in the string of palm trees that loomed outside, whose lazy branches lapped sunlight in strategic array but, in the end, sat unnoticed by passersby. With their perfect spacing, the trunks appeared victims of a transplant, carted to the side of a busy street to project an image of California perfection.

Jesse smirked. Even the trees were cosmetic.

Once he'd satisfied all his customer's questions, Jesse led her to the checkout counter with a handful of filters he doubted she'd ever use.

By eleven thirty in the morning, LensPerfection attracted its usual surge of foot traffic from those who took an early lunch hour. Most were browsers. A portrait studio sat toward the back and lured the occasional actor-to-be, who arrived with a designer coffee or vitamin water in hand, ready to schedule a shoot for the head shot that would make him famous.

Jesse's head shots were free. After several years of part-time employment, the owner allowed the extra perk and arranged Jesse's schedule around his bottom-rung work on film and television shoots. But the shoots had become sparse and, for two years straight, Jesse had not met the minimal hours required to secure medical coverage through his union. At this point, however, benefits were the least of his concerns.

Jesse's wavy, dark-blond hair, chiseled jaw line, and tall, fit form caught frequent second glances from both genders. But for Hollywood's cameras, handsome didn't seem to cut it, not when perfection stood next in line.

Jesse felt a vibration in his pocket. When he flipped his cell phone open and discovered a new text message from Maddy, his agent, his hopes surged. She had gotten word of a possible audition, a small supporting role in a feature film, and had pursued the prospect for weeks. Although it consisted of five lines, it represented an opportunity to expand his resume and connect with its director and principals. Jesse needed the gig.

And the audition was scheduled.

Emotional attachments are dangerous; better to take the

news in stride, but this audition could mark the official end of his dry spell and justify years of waiting in L.A.

Jesse returned his attention to the store and the hum of its electric doorbell. A customer, a man around forty years old, entered and hung his sunglasses on his shirt opening. Dressed in starched khakis and a perfect haircut, the man looked more like a mid-level executive who had stopped by on his way to a round of golf. Jesse wondered what a corporate job with steady hours must be like.

"Can I help you?"

"I tossed a roll of film in the drop-off bin yesterday." Jesse reached for the basket of completed photo packets on the rear counter. "Name?"

"Glen Merseal," he replied.

As Jesse flipped through packets, Glen fingered through some eight-by-tens stacked beside the cash register. When Jesse returned, Glen couldn't seem to pull himself away from a photo of a homeless man. In the photo, the subject leaned against a railing and gazed at the ocean, his face afire beneath a midday sun. With his fishing rod extended in search of a victim, the homeless man's face spoke of mystery. Jesse couldn't determine whether the subject appeared content or forlorn; perhaps the man struggled between the two.

Jesse began to ring out the order.

Glen tapped the edge of the photo with his finger and said, "This guy's expression intrigues me. The photographer captured his, what? His aura?"

"Oh, it's not a professional photo." Jesse chuckled. "It's just a sample photo to illustrate the paper quality."

"Do you know who took the picture?"

Jesse shoved a hand into his pocket. "I did." When Glen's

eyebrows rose a bit, Jesse added, "I shot that photo at the Santa Monica Pier. I've seen that man from time to time. Guy's name is Marshall. He must catch dinner there. Life on the beach, huh?"

"Did you take photography classes?"

"A high school class way back, but nothing else. I dabble in it here and there, flip through books to pick up tips. Trust me, I'm no professional."

"That's amazing." Glen glanced at the photo again, but this time he held it up to the light. He extended his hand. "What's your name?"

"Jesse. Nice to meet you."

As they shook hands, Glen reached for his wallet and removed a business card.

"My kid's got a birthday coming up. We're giving her a little party in a couple of weeks at a park nearby. Would you be interested in taking some action shots?"

"You're making a professional out of me, is that it?"

Glen nodded.

"Sure," Jesse said. "Who couldn't use the extra cash?"

If only film and television jobs were this easy to obtain.

"Great! We'll figure out the details letter. Number's on the card."

As the customer walked away, Jesse peered down at the business card. Was it possible Glen might work in the legal department at a studio?

No such luck. Glen was a franchise owner in a fast-food chain.

CHAPTER 3

JADA arrived home around six that night. No purse or keys on the breakfast-bar ledge above the kitchen counter, which meant Jada hadn't yet come home. He tried to recall her schedule today: Dinner plans with Barry Richert and a studio executive? Ink a deal to direct an adaptation of that recent book lauded by critics? He couldn't keep track of her life. By virtue of her job, Jada subjected herself to Barry's continual beck and call. Then again, Jesse was thankful to have the apartment to himself for the moment; nowadays her presence alone could trigger tension.

His eyes sensitive from the fluorescent lights at the shop, Jesse slid onto the black leather sofa in the living room and went limp for a few minutes. He ran his hand through his hair. Was he getting tired quicker? Though subtle, he had noticed a difference.

He stared at the jasmine candles on the coffee table, the ones from the previous night, his sinuses acute to the sharp scent. What is it with women and candles? he wondered. Jada wasn't the kind of woman to leave them at random spots around the apartment, however, so he counted his blessings. Subtle yet aggressive, she was the type to lay the bait and wait for someone to notice and respond with a compliment. And Jesse was grateful she chose a scent other than vanilla. Then again, Jada herself was anything but vanilla.

In its entirety, the apartment décor could be credited to Jada. The glass-top coffee table on a slab of generic gray stone, jazz wall prints fit for a coffee house, muted chrome lamps—everything possessed a contemporary nonchalance, as if an interior decorator stopped by on periodic visits and left behind articles much like you'd forget a ballpoint pen. Every element reflected Jada's personality. It was a far cry from the more traditional embellishments he found in his northern Ohio hometown. But to her credit, Jada had managed to frame a few of his photographs and put them on the bookshelves. Jesse held no strong opinions in the matter, though on occasion he felt like a stranger in his own home.

And, of course, the lease was in her name.

He grabbed his cell phone from his pocket and read Maddy's text message again. Countless months had passed since he'd heard good news; he had to savor this audition prospect. Most of Jesse's media work was as an extra, a random individual who walked down background corridors or pointed at superheroes that clung to the sides of buildings. Seldom did Jesse learn whether he appeared in the final cut until the film opened in theaters.

But he had never carried a line of dialogue. If successful, this audition would be a game changer. A small role, yet even award-winning celebrities had their minor moments early on: Richard Dreyfuss offered to call the police in The Graduate; Jodie Foster lent her voice to an animated Charlie Brown.

On the other hand, his confidence had taken a severe blow the last two years. It's said you shouldn't become an actor if you can't handle rejection. But while the initial rejections are heart-breaking, soon those rejections become routine, to which you grow impervious, like skin numbed by an ice cube. Jesse had always taken rejection in stride. Today, however, with his gears rusty, Jesse fought internal doubts about whether he could win this role. The way he saw it, the odds didn't fare well for him.

No. Forget the doubt, he thought. It's been too long. This has to work out. He didn't want to think about the alternative: another failure, another embarrassment, another step toward a terminated dream.

Jada didn't understand. Despite her industry savvy, she—

Jesse heard keys jingle outside. Speak of the devil.

She entered in a flourish. Without a greeting, Jada unleashed as soon as she spotted him on the couch.

"Can you believe the guy in the next building parked his crappy car in front of our doorway again? I had to walk halfway up the block to get here. My Beemer is worth more than that guy's gas pedal! What the fuck's the matter with him?"

A delicate body figure with a cast-iron tongue. Polished and professional on the job, though. Not an off-color word from her on the set. She knew who fed her and how to perform for an audience of her own.

Jada left her purse and keys on the breakfast bar, then plopped down on the sofa beside Jesse and kicked off her shoes. As Jesse massaged her knee, she drew her legs underneath her and tugged at a bracelet. "I hate location shoots," she said.

That's right, she spent today in Malibu. "That bad, huh?"

"Once the police got the street blocked off and we started rolling, it went fine. A side street off the 101. We shot a couple of short scenes in the morning to minimize our days outside the studio lot." In a single motion, her eyes lit up and she engaged her hands in a near pantomime. "Oh, then it got to be noon and the real fun started. You know those people who wander by and decide they want to make their screen debut? Someone peeks behind a building across the street? We got one of those."

"A side street in Malibu isn't what you'd call a high foot-traffic area."

"I don't know what this guy was thinking, but he's coy. Starts out on the 101, just walks by. Maybe a tourist who just had lunch."

"How far away were you from 101?"

"A couple of blocks, but he wanders up the sidewalk. No crime. He inches closer till he's a few feet away from the action." She leaned forward and spread her fingers toward Jesse. "Amanda Galley's starring in this thing, okay? So she's hanging out, flirting with the crew like she does. This tourist guy waddles up and makes a remark to her, thinks he's gonna score with this A-lister. Well, I don't know what he said to her; the story versions change depending on who you talk to. But he got assaulted with a shoe, and—"

"A shoe? How?"

"He got hit in the head with a shoe."

"Whose shoe?" "Amanda's! She's in costume, some riches-to-rags character, loses all her money and collects seashells by the seashore in her high heels. Anyway, she pulls off her shoe and hits the guy right in the middle of his forehead. Disaster. The guy doesn't know what hit him. He starts to scream when a trickle of blood runs down his nasty face. So now the police wander over to check it out, the guy says he's gonna sue, all this shit. Because he got nicked in the head by Amanda Galley's pink shoe. She'll probably show up on the news tonight. What a moron."

"Amanda or the guy?"

"Both of them. Have you ever worked with her?"

"No."

"Prima donna. And if you think about it, she's never had a big hit." In a huff Jada fell back against the sofa and drew her brunette hair to rest on her shoulders. Jesse found her olive, Mediterranean skin tone exotic.

Jada had had dreams of her own at one point. She grew up in Reno, Nevada, with her own mother as her biggest fan since infancy. As a preschooler, the talented Jada entered a long list of beauty pageants, where she performed a tap-dance routine with a cane and top hat, choreographed by her mom, a former dancer in Vegas. By first grade, Jada had appeared in a handful of local commercials and, when she was eight, landed a role on television: Bailey's Gang, a hip, educational program that started as a local Reno show and graduated to syndication during the mid 1980s. Jesse had heard the rundown countless times. Jada played one of a dozen Tree House Kids on the song-and-sketch show which was, in actuality, a rip-off of better-known pre-decessors—an admission Jada allowed because she considered herself the show's answer to Annette Funicello.

After five years on the air, controversy raged when a reporter photographed Bailey handing a beer to a Tree House Kid. The show entered hiatus and never recovered. Jada's acting career screeched to a halt, but still existed in the deep recesses of her subconscious. She seemed to long for those golden days and, due perhaps to unresolved childhood issues, seemed to remain a little girl at heart. When they first moved in together, Jesse discovered a secret stash of videotapes in Jada's closet—her favorite Bailey's Gang episodes. Jesse found the stash adorable, but when he took his discovery a step further and joked about her collection, Jada actually cried.

Jesse got up and headed for the kitchen. "I'll get you a beer, how's that?"

"No, I'll just have a glass of wine at dinner. Did you work at the shop today?"

"Yeah, a full day. Wasn't as eventful as yours, though."

"Nobody tried to steal a roll of film? No armed robbery?"

"Not quite," he called from the kitchen. "A customer hired me to shoot pictures at his kid's birthday party. A little extra cash."

Expressionless, Jada examined her manicured nails. "Gee, exciting stuff. I can see why you like it there."

Bottle of Budweiser in hand, Jesse walked back into the room and took a swig. He settled back on the sofa, rested his elbows on his knees as Jada moved closer. She ran her hand along his back.

"I heard from Maddy today," Jesse said as he picked at the bottle label. "She scheduled me for an audition."

"Which project?"

"Taking Sides. It's a bit part."

"The new Mark Shea project? Why would you want that?"

"I need the gig. What's wrong with it?"

"He's lost his vision. His last three films tanked. He cast a sinking star in the lead role. You want to associate yourself with that? How many times have I explained this to you?"

"Look, it's not like I have a choice. I don't work for Barry Richert, who picks his projects."

"How many others are up for the part?"

"Four or five. Maddy doesn't have many specifics on it; she just knows they want someone tall."

"Well, you should have a decent shot at it." A quick pause before Jada swung her head around to face him eye to eye.

"What else is going on? You've got those lines in your fore-head—the ones you get when you're worried."

For a moment, Jesse traced his finger along the permanent crease line of his khaki pants, where the fabric had lightened a shade. He shrugged.

"Do you ever feel like you've lost your edge?" he asked.

"Like what, risk-taking?"

He waved at her reply. "More like your momentum—that bold side of you that drives you to face the odds."

"Have you forgotten who you sleep next to?" Jada searched his eyes, but furrowed her eyebrows when Jesse remained stone-faced. To her, he must have looked like he studied the ether that hovered over the coffee table. In truth, Jesse knew she didn't have a clue what motivated him. Nor did she care, as long as his motivation existed. "You aren't afraid of that audition, are you?" she asked.

"After as many as I've been on? Granted, not lately—"

"Because if you are scared," she continued, "you need figure out a way to hide it. Or else you'll never get that role." She chuckled to herself. Jada shook her head, then plopped back against the sofa and crossed her arms. "Don't you want to be an actor anymore?"

"Now you've forgotten who you sleep next to. Why would you even ask that?"

"Things change."

Great, now she's in challenge mode. Jesse clenched his jaw, threw his hands on his head in frustration. "Dammit, Jada! Nothing's changed!" After a deep breath, he let his hands fall to his sides. Why did he try to talk to her about this? Of all people, she would be the last to understand unless the struggle was her own. "Forget it."

For the first time in L.A., Jesse felt alone.

Weary, he turned to Jada and looked into her eyes. With a gentle rub to her back, he said, "Sorry, babe. It's nothing. Jitters."

But he could pinpoint the suspicion in her autumn eyes. When it came to fear detection, the woman had radar.

Jesse leaned in and planted a kiss on her lips.

He'd always adored her Italian lips.

CPSIA information can be obtained at www.ICGtesting.com
Printed in the USA
LVOW120236140213

320058LV00001B/15/P